Dicky Star and the garden rule

Tony White

Dicky Star and the garden rule
By Tony White
Commissioned by Forma
ISBN 978-0-9548288-6-8
© Tony White, 2012

Published by Forma Arts and Media Ltd
4-8 Scrutton Street
London
EC1V 4RT
www.forma.org.uk

Designed by Valerie Norris

Published to coincide with
Atomgrad (Nature Abhors a Vacuum), **Jane and Louise Wilson**
Commissioned by Forma, in association with John Hansard Gallery,
Dundee Contemporary Arts and The Whitworth Art Gallery,
University of Manchester. Supported by Arts Council England.
Project research supported by the British Council, Ukraine
and the Center for Urban History of Central East Europe, Lviv.

...and so they are casting their problems on society and who is society? There is no such thing! There are individual men and women and there are families and no government can do anything except through people and people look to themselves first. It is our duty to look after ourselves […]

There is no such thing as society.

Margaret Thatcher speaking to Douglas Keay for Woman's Own *magazine in an interview published 31 October 1987 under the title, 'Aids, education and the year 2000!'* [i]

Saturday April 26 1986

'Okay, hun, if you're so clever. Four down. "Barrel-stand."[ii] L something, N something, R something.'

    '*Barrel*-stand? No; no idea. *Barrel*? I didn't know they had stands.'

    'Or how about this. Five down: "Feelers."[iii]'

    'Like an insect? Antennae[1]!'

    'No, it's *O* something. T something, N something, A something.'

    '*O* something? Are you sure?' Laura snatched the newspaper out of Jeremy's hands. It had been folded inside out – the back cover brought around to meet the front in order to expose the inside back page, home of the classifieds, of cartoons by Gary Trudeau and Steve Bell, and of the two daily crosswords – then folded in half and in half again. The Quick Crossword and all the white space around it was covered in a blue biro scrawl of answers and workings out. 'That's not how you spell "seismologist". It's only got one L.'

    'In that case,' said Jeremy, 'it's a mistake. There's one space too many.'

    'Or maybe the clue should have been "Bovine earthquake expert?" Ha! Why don't you come down?'

    'But it's got to be seismollogist! Look, one across: "Earthquake expert."[iv] It's seis..., okay, one L, seismologist. What else could it be? Look "seismo-" fits. One down: "Notice [dash] diocese." That's "see[2]," right, which also fits with two across, "entrain[3]"? Two down is "intense[4]," so, S something, I something. Then three down must be "mean[5]." Which gives us S something, I something M, -*ologist*. Bloody *Grauniad*!"

    'Oh, yeah, right, that must be it! There's a mistake in the crossword! But look, even with one L, seismologist wouldn't work because five down is definitely "antennae." No way it would be something starting with a G. Don't you fancy a snog in the back row?'

    'I just wish you didn't have to work every Saturday. Can't someone else do it?'

    'I don't get a grant, remember. And it's easy money doing the student shift. Why don't you come down? You know I can get you in for free.'

    'I may[6] do, but I'm always too tired by then. Anyway, what's on?'

    '"Too tired"! I can't remember. Look it up. Got *Leeds Other Paper* somewhere.'

    'Can't they do another Cary Grant season? That was great.'

---

[1]   5 down: 'Feelers (8).' Quick Crossword 5,003. *The Guardian*, 26 April 1986

[2]   1 down: 'Notice – diocese (3).' #5003. *Ibid.*

[3]   8 across: 'Board for rail journey (7).' #5,003. *Ibid.*

[4]   2 down: 'Concentrated (7).' #5,003. *Ibid.*

[5]   3 down: 'Intend – average (4).' #5,003. *Ibid.*

[6]   23 down: 'Month (3).' #5,003. *Ibid.*

'Is that all you want to watch: Cary Grant films?'

'It's how I met you.'

'At the late night screening...'

'*Bringing Up Baby*. We got there early. You were working behind the bar.'

'Yes I remember. You were both so stoned, I should have... Anyway, I thought you were gay.'

'Yeah, so you said. You didn't know that Cary Grant was an acid-head!'

'No, it wasn't that.'

'A hero of the psychedelic counterculture!'

'Your ambition! No it was your slightly camp interest in...'

'Pulp fiction! I was reading *Confessions of a Night Nurse*[7] by Rosie Dixon, and you looked at it and said, "Ooh, 'Gregory Isaacs: the untold story'!" Christ! That was nearly a year ago.'

'Do you think you might be, you know, *awake* when I get back? Or will you have "fallen asleep" in front of the snooker like every other night this week? Impossible to stir[8]. You never used to watch telly all the time.'

'That's because I didn't have one! It's your telly! I carried it all the way from Cardigan Road.'

'Like a thief[9]!'

'And you, a brunette[10] come to share my bunk[11]!'

'You stole my heart. You and your continental quilt.'

'Anyway, I like the snooker.'

'In black and white? You do know they only started putting snooker on when colour telly was invented? Someone at college told me. "The reason being," he said, "because colour is what is at stake." Ah,' she tapped the folded newspaper with the point of the biro. 'Okay, I get it. Look: "Pull up"[v] has got to be "hoist[12]," right? Five letters. And "Mirror-like surface,"[vi] something something F, something E... Something like "reflect"? Reflector[13] fits. Which means it ends in R. So it's "seismo-" something something A, something H, something R.'

'You're a natural[14].'

'I know; and I didn't even have any breakfast[15]. It ends in E-R then I bet. E-R as in Exeter[16], or mother!'

---

7   18 down: 'Tend (5).' #5,003. *Ibid.*

8   19 across: 'Cause a commotion (4).' #5,003. *Ibid.*

9   8 across: '"Punctuality is the _____ of time" (Wilde) (5).' #5,003. *Ibid.*

10   11 across: 'Dark haired woman (8).' #5,003. *Ibid.*

11   10 across: 'Sleeping berth (4).' #5,003. *Ibid.*

12   6 down: 'Pull up (5).' #5,003. *Ibid.*

13   7 down: 'Mirror-like surface (9).' #5,003. *Ibid.*

14   15 down: 'Unaltered (eg by industrial development) (7).' #5,003. *Ibid.*

15   10 down: 'Meal (9).' #5,003. *Ibid.*

16   13 across: 'SW Cathedral and University city (6).' #5,003. *Ibid.*

'You can leave my family out of it, but yes, I see. As in retainer[17]!'

'As in *sever* all connections; apron[18] strings included. So, theoretically[19]... Oh, I love this song. Might have to borrow the tape when I go, that okay?'

'Course.'

'What is it again?'

'You always ask me that. It's This Mortal Coil.'

'The song?'

'The band. The song is "Kangaroo[20]", see?'

'It always reminds me of some train journey in a French film. Walnut[21] trees sliding past the window, scratches on the counter of a buffet car, zinc[22] as grey and luminous as a Solent[23] mist. Subtitled dialogue reduced to a series of pointless and mysterious epigrams – untranslatable. Don't you want to come?'

'Maybe I do. If it was *that* film. I could get in to that.'

'Washed-out photography. Hey! Could a *gantry*[24] be a kind of barrel-stand? Because if so it could be -ographer rather than -ologist.'

'Really? Such a thing as a seismographer[25]?'

'I reckon.'

'Brilliant! Okay, here's an epigram[26] for you: "When the crossword's complete, it's time for a treat." Do you think it's too early for a...?' He rubbed both thumbs and forefingers together in a gentle rolling motion a biro's length apart. Raised his eyebrows enticingly, he thought.

'It is for me, but I'd love a coffee. Bit of *Brookside*, then I'll have to go.' She held up the paper: 'Have you finished with this? In case it's quiet. That Dungeness thing. Did you see it? Been broken for years, apparently, but everyone was too embarrassed to admit it! I wanted to show CND Steve.'

'Oh Christ!' said Jeremy, reaching for the Rizla whilst imitating the apologetic grimace and earnest inflection of Laura's Leeds Playhouse co-worker: '"...*and he's not wearing a collar because he's a friend and not a slave!*" If Steve's on, I definitely won't be coming down. Love a tea though, if you're making one.'

---

17 12 down: 'Servant (8).' #5,003. *Ibid.*

18 21 across: 'Protective garment (5).' #5,003. *Ibid.*

19 24 across: 'According to existing speculations (13).' #5,003. *Ibid.*

20 17 across: 'Type of apple, court or rat (8).' #5,003. *Ibid.*

21 14 across: 'Light brown (wood) (6).' #5,003. *Ibid.*

22 20 down: 'Metallic element (4).' #5,003. *Ibid.*

23 16 down: 'It separates England from the Isle of Wight (6).' #5,003. *Ibid.*

24 4 down: 'Barrel-stand (6).' #5,003. *Ibid.*

25 1 across: 'Earthquake expert (13).' #5,003. *Ibid.*

26 22 across: 'Pointed satirical saying (7).' #5,003. *Ibid.*

Monday April 28 1986

'What was I saying? Oh yeah, and Dr. Morbius is Prospero[27]! Can't believe you haven't seen it!' continued Jeremy as he joined Laura and their shopping at the counter of the Playhouse bar and cafe, then: 'Hi, Steve. Um, there's no bog roll in the gents.'

'Alright, Jez. Ooh, thanks. I'll get on to that.' Steve turned back to Laura: 'Yeah, and so meanwhile the human race is blasted back to the Iron Age[28], and they're all safely tucked away in some subterranean hideout[29] in the Ural[30]...'

'He hates being called Jez, don't you.'

'Ah, sorry!' said Steve.

'Yeah, it reminds me of school. Listening to Dire Straits[31] at the end of term, you know. Catchphrases from the *Dick Emery*[32] *Show*. The smell of hymn books and trying to pick a loose thread on your kneeler[33]. The whole petty[34]...'

'I know what you mean, Jeremy,' said Steve, conscientiously. 'It was always, "Hit me with your rhythm stick" at my school: "Eskimo and kakapo[35]." Our English teacher was a fan. Put me right off.'

Noticing Jeremy's features beginning to assume what she thought of as his 'muso' sneer – to the unpleasantness of which only he was oblivious – Laura had to move quickly: 'While you were in the loo, Steve was just saying we should get more involved. We've missed a load of stuff in the last couple of weeks: the Worldwide Nuclear Weapons Roll-call in Dortmund Square, Menwith Hill *and* the Star Wars talk.'

'Aye, I saw them in last week's *LOP*.' The sneer came anyway, then, but in diluted form: 'What? To meet kindred[36] spirits and oppose the crafty[37] killer[38] on an *ad hoc*[39] basis?'

'Too right!' said Steve, totally convinced by his own lack of eloquence. 'Unless[40] you've got something better to do! Anyway, before I launch headlong[41]

---

[27] 17 across: 'Character in The Tempest (8).' Quick Crossword 5,004. *The Guardian*, 28 April 1986
[28] 13 down: 'Historical period (4, 3).' #5,004. *Ibid.*
[29] 5 down: 'Retreat (7).' #5,004. *Ibid.*
[30] 9 across: 'Mountain in Russian range (4).' #5,004. *Ibid.*
[31] 12 across: 'Extreme poverty (4, 7).' #5,004. *Ibid.*
[32] 22 across: 'Hard mineral (5).' #5,004. *Ibid.*
[33] 2 down: 'Hassock (7).' #5,004. *Ibid.*
[34] 18 down: 'Small-minded (5).' #5,004. *Ibid.*
[35] 1 across: 'NZ owl-parrot (6).' #5,004. *Ibid.*
[36] 1 down: 'Relations (7).' #5,004. *Ibid.*
[37] 20 across: 'Wily (6).' #5,004. *Ibid.*
[38] 21 across: 'Murderer (6).' #5,004. *Ibid.*
[39] 4 across: 'For this purpose (2, 3).' #5,004. *Ibid.*
[40] 7 across: 'If not (6).' #5,004. *Ibid.*
[41] 10 across: 'Precipitately (8).' #5,004. *Ibid.*

into why you should join *post-haste*[42], what can I get you?'

'Um,' said Jeremy, turning to Laura as if she knew what he wanted.

'Listen,' said Steve, taking advantage, 'you've got to *try* and change[43] things, then at least you can say you've acted[44].'

'Don't bother, Steve. Jeremy's too stingy[45] to join anything. He moans about spending 20p on *Leeds Other Paper*, but show him a second hand Michael Moorcock novel... Um, one tea one coffee. Any of that flapjack left from the weekend?'

'It's 30p,' said Jeremy.

'The flapjack?'

'*Leeds Other Paper*. 30p. Used to be twenty, but it's gone up.'

'Listen,' said Steve. 'It makes a difference. If people hadn't protested they'd still be using stadia[46]... *stadiums* as death camps in Chile or where-ever. It's the same with...'

'Nucular?' said Laura, habitually.

'Weapons, yeah. That's what Greenham's all about. Menwith Hill. The peace camps. We've got to let Reagan know that they simply can't do whatever the fuck they want! Look at the way they attacked Libya a couple of weeks ago. It's not them that's in the firing line for that, it's us! We're nothing but an aircraft carrier to them. *And* Thatcher's letting them get away with it. Christ! If the Tories get their way with this new Public Order Bill, it'll be illegal to even protest about it. And even if they did allow you to protest, if you said something they didn't like they'd do you for disorderly conduct or whatever; silence you that way! So if we don't make a fuss while we can it'll be all Apache[47] helicopters at dawn or whatever.'

'I s'pose,' Jeremy conceded.

'Definitely. And when the yanks are shifting that many fully armed cruise missiles around, you don't have to be some kind of seer[48] to know it's only a matter of time before, I don't know, a B52 hits an air-pocket[49], or you know, a pilot forgets his insulin[50] and presses something by accident, and BOOM! Good bye leafy English scenery[51], hello lunar landscape! Sorry, anyway,' Steve said, remembering the job in hand. 'Two teas, was it?'

'One coffee, one tea.'

'Take a seat. I'll bring them over.'

---

42   3 down: 'Immediate (4-5).' #5,004. *Ibid.*
43   6 down: 'Modify (6).' #5,004. *Ibid.*
44   4 down: 'Played a part (5).' #5,004. *Ibid.*
45   23 across: 'Mean (6).' #5,004. *Ibid.*
46   8 across: 'Sports grounds (6).' #5,004. *Ibid.*
47   16 down: 'Red Indian (6).' #5,004. *Ibid.*
48   19 across: 'Prophet (4).' #5,004. *Ibid.*
49   11 down: 'Region of danger for flyers (3-6).' #5,004. *Ibid.*
50   14 down: 'Product of pancreas (7).' #5,004. *Ibid.*
51   15 down: 'Theatrical set (7).' #5,004. *Ibid.*

'Thanks Steve,' said Laura, pointing out a table in the corner, before turning back to ask: 'Flapjacks?'

'God, he's so annoying,' Jeremy said, organising the Morrison's carrier bags on the floor next to his chair a few moments later. 'It's not kakapo, it's Arapaho.'

'What are you talking about?'

'"Hit me with your rhythm stick." It's not "Eskimo and *kakapo*," it's "Eskimo, Arapaho."'

'What?'

'I think that a kakapo,' Jeremy said, impatiently, 'is some kind of flightless parrot.'

'And what is an Arapaho, as if I cared?'

'I don't know: a red indian?'

'Jeremy!' Laura only half-joked: 'That's *so* politically unsound!'

Tuesday April 29 1986

'Listen to this,' said Laura, scanning the front page of *The Guardian* newspaper that Jeremy had picked up at the newsagents after his fortnightly walk down to the Post Office. 'At least the Swedes have read the manual[52]! Blah, blah, yes, here it is: workers at some nucular power station in Sweden were evacuated, because they thought *they* had a leak, before... Hang on, I'll just read it out, "...before it became clear that the radioactive plume was drifting in across the Baltic."[vii]'

'I know, I read it on the way home!' said Jeremy. 'I nearly walked into a lamp post down in the Brudenells; completely forgot about the samosas! I liked that bit about the Swedish authorities *immediately* broadcasting radio warnings, telling people to keep away from the area, before they realised that it wasn't them after all! Can you imagine that here? Do you think the authorities here would be so candid, so voluble[53]?'

'Radio broadcasts! No chance,' Laura laughed. 'Like the thing in the paper on Saturday, remember? Did I show you? Turns out Dungeness or somewhere has been operating with broken turbines for years. It was only when some whistleblower leaked it...'

'Leaking the leak!' interrupted Jeremy, delightedly seizing the opportunity to make a bad pun.

She'd heard worse, but faced with her boyfriend's habitual impetuosity[54] on matters humorous, Laura sometimes thought that it was as if Jeremy's be-all[55]

---

[52]   1 across: 'Hand-(book) (6).' Quick Crossword 5,005. *The Guardian*, 29 April 1986
[53]   18 across: 'Copious in speech (7).' #5,005. *Ibid.*
[54]   13 across: 'Rashness (11).' #5,005. *Ibid.*
[55]   20 across: '(and 24) complete essence (2-3).' #5,005. *Ibid.*

and end-all[56] was to seek the joke in any given utterance, whether that joke might be funny or not and regardless of the seriousness of the conversation. Were all men like that? It sometimes seemed so. Bad enough Jeremy on his own, too, but when there were a few of them you could be forgiven for thinking that conversation in general was nothing more than a competition to see who could make everyone else laugh the most: intelligence reduced to little more than a pretext for the manic[57] pursuit of flattery-by-laughter.

'Steve will be beside himself,' said Jeremy. 'A flurry[58] of vindication, and then on with the struggle! I think he sees you as a potential apostle[59]. You know that, don't you.'

Laura allowed a flicker of a smile, a half-laugh, then pressed on: 'If workers at Dungeness B detected higher radiation levels, do you think the first thing they would do would be to broadcast radio warnings, or evacuate Kent?'

Jeremy shook his head with a light snort.

'Of course not,' Laura went on. 'The first reaction here would be to lie about it! No, they would keep it a secret[60]!'

Laura tried to imagine the kind of vast machinery that would creak into operation if a British government, or worse, a Tory one, were forced to respond to a similar situation: unexpectedly high radioactivity readings at a UK installation. It was enough to bring her out in a cold sweat[61]. Instead of Scandinavian openness, all she could imagine was hushed meetings, old boy networks, powerful friendships forged and old debts incurred in cloistered subfusc[62], civil servants colluding with ministers and armed forces; the secret service.

These kind of thoughts did more than unnerve[63] Laura, they terrified her, and the reason they did so was because it seemed that once the authorities set off down this path there didn't seem to be very many steps from state fraudulence[64] to state violence. Wasn't this supposed to be, after all, an evil that had been seen to bloom on the most unlikely of doorsteps? The coldness of it. Violence borne of expediency not rancour[65]. Hadn't Hilda Murrell, the rose grower and anti-nuclear campaigner been murdered by persons unknown? And others too, sacrificed it would seem on the altar[66] of, what? Banal[67] privilege and vested interest? And no matter the official protestations, talk of bad apples or one-offs. The terrifying truth seemed

---

[56] 24 across: 'See 20 across (3-3).' #5,005. *Ibid.*
[57] 10 across: 'Morbidly elated (5).' #5,005. *Ibid.*
[58] 17 down: 'Burst of activity (or snow?) (6).' #5,005. *Ibid.*
[59] 3 down: 'Champion (of the church) (7).' #5,005. *Ibid.*
[60] 7 down: 'Private (6).' #5,005. *Ibid.*
[61] 11 across: 'Perspiration (5).' #5,005. *Ibid.*
[62] 15 down: 'Dull in colour (7).' #5,005. *Ibid.*
[63] 12 across: 'Deprive of resolution (7).' #5,005. *Ibid.*
[64] 8 down: 'Criminal dishonesty (11).' #5,005. *Ibid.*
[65] 9 across: 'Spite and bitterness (7).' #5,005. *Ibid.*
[66] 21 down: 'Place of sacrifice (or marriage?) (5).' #5,005. *Ibid.*
[67] 19 down: 'Commonplace (5).' #5,005. *Ibid.*

to be that it was never just for the nonce[68], but a repeated pattern, a habit. Secret policies. Shoot to kill. And not just in Northern Ireland, although at least the Stalker enquiry would shortly, finally, be exposing one such scurvy[69] sore on the British body politic.

'Secrecy, yes, you're right,' said Jeremy. 'And if it happened here, if there *was* a major leak, *another one*, I'm sure the bastards would let us learn[70] about it later; the hard way. Wait for the cancer cluster[71] to appear before admitting anything.'

'Or lying even then, more like.'

'Yes. They'd cut down a forest so they could say it never existed! It's almost as if they're daring you to go and point out the tree stumps[72].'

'No,' said Laura. 'Well, *yes*, absolutely, but no, I was just thinking that if it happened here, if Dungeness went up, they'd just change the name to something rural-sounding or nondescript.'

'They tried that with Sellafield, though,' Jeremy frowned. 'Didn't work, did it. We all know it's still really Windscale.'

'Yeah, you're right,' said Laura, and he was. 'OK, then. This time they'd have to change it to something more, I don't know, friendly!'

'What,' asked Jeremy, remembering the holiday story of a childhood friend, 'like the "Romney, Hythe and Dymchurch Electrical Generating Company"?'

They both laughed.

'Yes,' said Laura. 'That'll do it. But only if the 'and' was written as an ampersand: Romney, Hythe,' she drew a figure in the air, '& Dymchurch! To make it look even more old-fashioned.'

'What's an amper-what?'

'Ampersand. The "and" symbol; on your typewriter! You know! It looks like something from the name of a Victorian shop.'

They both sat there for a few minutes, suddenly weighed down by the enormity of it all. Jeremy looked morose[73].

'Who is this?' Laura asked halfheartedly, as if looking for any distraction.

'It's The Clash. *Sandinista.*'

'Doesn't sound like The Clash.'

'No,' said Jeremy, 'it's a different singer just on this one track: Tymon Dogg.'

'Like Timon[74] of Athens? What's the minaret[75] one that I like?'

---

68   2 down: '(for the) moment (5).' #5,005. *Ibid.*
69   25 across: 'Contemptible – disease (6).' #5,005. *Ibid.*
70   22 across: 'Acquire knowledge (5).' #5,005. *Ibid.*
71   23 across: 'Group, e.g. of stars (7).' #5,005. *Ibid.*
72   4 across: 'Constituents of wicket (6).' #5,005. *Ibid.*
73   1 down: 'Sullen (6).' #5,005. *Ibid.*
74   5 down: 'Misanthropic Athenian (5).' #5,005. *Ibid.*
75   6 down: 'Turret in mosque (7).' #5,005. *Ibid.*

'"Rock the Casbah,"' said Jeremy. 'On *Combat Rock*. I've got the cassette somewhere.'

Laura had heard Jeremy's Clash story that many times that she knew she could tell it better than he did, so they sat in silence again for a few minutes until finally it was Laura who spoke.

'Or maybe that's just not enough any more,' she suggested. 'To change the name. The Windscale trick!'

'What do you mean, my svelte[76] one?' asked Jeremy, winsomely.

'Well, if that *did* happen, maybe they'd have to try and displace Dungeness altogether; completely change the story. Reduce the importance of the power station in the public imagination. Make the nucular issue subservient to something a bit more *cuddly*.'

She thought for a few seconds: 'They'd have to make Dungeness the backdrop to something – I don't know – very *nostalgic*, and as British as a china mallard[77]: those ducks on Hilda Ogden's living room wall! No, that's not it. Maybe something less kitsch, but even more distracting: a traditional craft come domestic displacement activity like *baking*, or jam-making, or, I don't know, something along those lines.'

Wednesday April 30 1986

Laura was starting to worry about Jeremy almost as much as she was starting to worry about events in and around the Soviet Socialist Republic of Ukraine. She knew that her boyfriend and she were sometimes as bad as each other and could egg each other on something chronic. There was the time they had found a kitchen knife on the gas meter[78] and spent a night of terror convinced that their office worker neighbour was a serial killer, before accepting the more obvious explanation that he had been trying to raid the meter's cash box. Thankfully though, this time Laura had managed to talk herself down, to restrain[79] the initially persuasive prospect that some unspecified major accident at Dungeness would be proven not by state admission, but by media collusion in the production of a new myth about the area, a story of self-sacrifice based on the all-too-English activity of gardening, of all things!

It had all seemed so convincing the night before. Laura had called it 'the garden rule' and Jeremy hadn't needed much persuading. They'd even got as far as wondering who might be the face of such a myth: the nuclear gardener. Someone off the telly? It almost felt close enough to touch! A charismatic rock star, say, or TV

---

76   16 down: 'Lissom (6).' #5,005. *Ibid.*
77   14 down: 'Wild duck (7).' #5,005. *Ibid.*
78   18 across: 'Stem rage (anag) (3, 5).' Quick Crossword 5,006. *The Guardian*, 30 April 1986
79   12 across: 'Check (time off – wet weather!) (8).' #5,006. *Ibid.*

presenter, but one who might be accepting of the curtailment that such a trammel[80] would bring: life in the goldfish bowl.

'Let's call him "Dicky Star",' suggested Jeremy, invoking a variety show archetype, 'the generic entertainer.'

Would the victim go happily, they had asked themselves, into so dramatic and self-sacrificial a last posting? An army[81] background, they had decided, was a must. Dicky would have some intimate and familial knowledge of danger, but also be possessed of an old-fashioned, 'mind how you go[82]' politeness: a real hail fellow well met[83].

But now, slightly numbed and thick-headed still as she was, and walking to college between the grammar school and the park on this beautiful sunny morning, listening to *It'll End in Tears* on the Walkman and with a paperback of *Humboldt's Gift* in her bag, those particular fears seemed to have evaporated: it really had just been the dope talking. A mid-morning seminar about Saul Bellow[84] entitled 'Hoist[85] on its own petard? Culture and commodity in the post-war period' was just what she needed to take her mind off things.

The truth was that Laura's own anxiety had been abruptly and genuinely displaced, rendered more prosaic and family-focused by the news relayed that morning in the first letter she had ever received from her usually taciturn[86] and rather straightedge[87] older brother, Edward. She hadn't even recognised his writing, just the GU8 postmark. This sudden, veritable loquaciousness on his part was prompted, as she learned, by the disturbing fact that their parents were currently on holiday on the Turkish Black Sea coast near Trabzon, on what was in fact the first holiday abroad they had ever taken on their own: what were the chances? Edward said it was one of those coach holidays, two days here, three days there, and however shaky her grasp of matters geographical, Laura knew that Chernobyl was closer to Turkey than it was to Chiddingfold.

As she waited to cross Clarendon Road, she noticed a pigeon pecking at the chewed up remains of half a Mars bar in the gutter near her feet. Laura hated pigeons: she could almost actually smell their greasy feathers. 'Shoo[88]!' she said, gagging slightly and waving her hands in its general direction. Then, aware in spite of this momentary distraction that the lights had changed, she stepped off the kerb only to find one foot and her whole self suddenly and inexplicably rooted to the spot:

---

[80]   2 down: 'Fishing net – hamper (7).' #5,006. *Ibid.*
[81]   3 down: 'Military unit (4).' #5,006. *Ibid.*
[82]   24 across: 'Watch your step? (4, 3, 3, 2).' #5,006. *Ibid.*
[83]   14 across: ' "_____ by moonlight, proud Titania" (M.N.D.) (3, 3).' (second part). #5,006. *Ibid.*
[84]   17 down: 'Loud shout (6).' #5,006. *Ibid.*
[85]   23 across: 'Raise or lift (5).' #5,006. *Ibid.*
[86]   5 down: 'Of few words (8).' #5,006. *Ibid.*
[87]   1 across: 'Ruler (12).' #5,006. *Ibid.*
[88]   21 down: 'Go away! (4).' #5,006. *Ibid.*

her right heel had wedged itself into a storm drain grating[89]. It was so embarrassing having to sit on the kerb and take her shoe off – trapped as she was in the pigeon's foul aura and unable to hold her breath – but the heel was wedged in so tightly that it took another whole cycle of the traffic lights to coax it out.

Jeremiah[90], as his friends called him at such times, was prone to episodes of eccentricity[91] and slight paranoia, but the latter was usually focused either on the fact that around Giro day he was more or less certain to be in possession of a quarter of an ounce of the best hash that his friend Dave had to offer and thus keeping an eye out for the old bill[92], or – and the two things were not unrelated – to be so stoned that he was rendered unable to speak. But this was different. Something about the 'disaster'[viii], the word had finally been used in the paper that morning, really seemed to be getting to him, and Laura had noticed that Jeremy was starting to gibber[93] a little in conversation, to be a bit speedy, something that she'd only seen him do once before, when they had been coming up on mushrooms a little too quickly and had got lost in some stone-housed-suburban-allotment-alleyway-hell whilst trying to find their way from an Otley bus stop to the end of the road and up on to the moor. She had fleetingly wondered if he wasn't perhaps becoming ill[94].

Laura didn't know that as soon as she had left, Jeremy skinned up and made a strong cup of Nescafé, then got his prized, Oxfam-purchased *Times Atlas* out from under the tea trolley that housed his record player. Laying it on the carpet he opened it at the relevant page for the East European Plain, which he could see stretched from Poland in the west to Arctic Russia in the north and – via a myriad of other Soviet Socialist Republics – Ukraine, on the opposite coast of the Black Sea from where Laura had just said her parents were staying in Turkey. By comparing this detailed map with the tiny one on the front page of the previous day's *Guardian* – which showed a teardrop-shaped radioactive plume spreading north across Europe like sump[95] oil oozing slow and thick across a garage floor – he could see that Chernobyl was in the north of the Ukrainian Soviet Socialist Republic, between capital Kiev and the border with the Belorussian SSR. Jeremy followed the line of the Dnieper River down through to its delta[96] on the Black Sea and tried to imagine what fallout looked like – talc[97]? – and whether radiation burns made you look like Freddie Kruger[98] from the *Nightmare on Elm Street* movie. He tried to picture the actor in his

---

[89]   16 down: 'Grille – harsh in sound! (7).' #5,006. *Ibid.*
[90]   13 down: 'Gloomy prophet (8).' #5,006. *Ibid.*
[91]   7 down: 'Oddness (12).' #5,006. *Ibid.*
[92]   22 across: 'World War I cartoon character – police! (3, 4).' #5,006. *Ibid.*
[93]   4 down: 'Talk like ghost or monkey (6).' #5,006. *Ibid.*
[94]   14 across: ' "_____ by moonlight, proud Titania" (M.N.D.) (3, 3).' (first part). #5,006. *Ibid.*
[95]   11 across: 'Reservoir for oil (4).' #5,006. *Ibid.*
[96]   6 down: 'Triangular area of river outlets (5).' #5,006. *Ibid.*
[97]   20 across: 'Mineral for powder (4).' #5,006. *Ibid.*
[98]   15 across: 'Boer president (6).' #5,006. *Ibid.*

dressing-room[99] and wondered how long it took to put on the make up, the prosthetic or whatever it was. He had a picture somewhere, cut out of a magazine. Where was it? He'd been using it as a bookmark.

Before Laura had gone to college, Jeremy had popped out for milk and the morning paper. On the way back he'd swung past Bobat's and bought a roll of masking tape. Now, with the place to himself he was cutting articles out of the last few day's newspapers: the Chernobyl coverage plus anything else that caught his eye or might be connected in some way. He put the roll of masking tape around his wrist like a bracelet to save time, then started sticking the cuttings on the wall, standing on the sofa to do so, and re-reading some of them as he went.

'Reactor region evacuated'[ix] read what Jeremy remembered from his school newspaper days was called the 'standfirst' above the main headline. But it was another of the front page articles in that day's paper that really caught his eye: 'Silence covers "zone of death"',[x] in column four.

Something about this felt as familiar as last night's dream, but he couldn't figure out why it gave him such a heightened feeling of *deja vu*. Where had he heard about this 'zone of death' before? Was it at some long-ago-attended CND talk about the neutron bomb, the device that was supposedly capable of killing all living things in range with a single, enormous burst of radiation whilst leaving the buildings intact? Maybe it was something of that which had persisted, but then he suddenly remembered the image of a beautiful woman who was being transported in a sedan[100] chair through just such a lifeless zone by a legion of the dead... *Christ!*

Jeremy dropped the newspaper and ran to the shelves near the window. It didn't take him long to find what he was looking for among his few dozen books: *The War Hound and the World's Pain*, a Michael Moorcock novel which, he knew, opened with the anti-hero Von Bek – an 18th century manifestation of Moorcock's 'Eternal Champion' – fleeing the bloodshed of post-revolutionary Paris only to find himself in an enchanted forest, where it seemed that nothing lived.

Jeremy pulled the book from the shelf and flicked through the first few pages, running his finger down the lines of print until he found the passage he was looking for. Here it was: having escaped a near ambush at the fording point of a river, Von Bek reports that as he rode deeper and deeper in to this seemingly bucolic[101] realm[102] the realisation dawned upon him that nothing lived. 'Few birds sang here: I saw no animals.' He realises that this was, 'not, after all, a paradise, but the borderland between Earth and Hell,'[xi] and concludes,

> that some natural catastrophe had driven the animal kingdom away,
> be it through famine or disease, and that it had not yet returned.

---

[99]   8 down: 'Changing place (8-4).' #5,006. *Ibid.*
[100]   19 down: 'Chair – battle (5).' #5,006. *Ibid.*
[101]   10 across: 'Rustic (7).' #5,006. *Ibid.*
[102]   9 across: 'Kingdom (5).' #5,006. *Ibid.*

Jeremy turned the page impatiently and continued reading until he came to a passage that seemed to him to be approaching the heart of the matter. Breaking into a clearing at the centre of the forest, Von Bek tells that he,

> saw before me [...] the most beautiful castle I had ever beheld: a thing of delicate stonework, of spires and ornamental battlements, all soft, pale browns, whites and yelllows, and this castle seemed to me to be at the centre of the silence, casting its influence for miles around...'[xiii]

Aghast, Jeremy turned to a blurred photo of Chernobyl that he had cut from the front page of that morning's paper and taped on to the living room wall. It was the first image of the power station that he had seen and it looked like a bad photocopy so it was hard to make anything out. A caption stated that the photograph had been taken from, 'the February edition of *Soviet Life* magazine.'[xiv]

A beautiful castle? It would certainly be as secure as a fortress, although there was not much to strike the Western eye as ornamental. That concrete, Jeremy thought, might be mistaken for pale brown stonework; that chimney and its delicate exoskeleton might seem a spire! But it was definitely right at, 'the centre of the silence,' that was for sure.

As Jeremy read, Von Bek continued:

> Yet it was mad to think such a thing, I knew. How could a building demand calm, to the degree that not even a mosquito would disturb it.[xvi]

Jeremy suddenly felt nauseous and unsteady on his feet as a kind of psychic vertigo washed through his body. Was *The Warhound and the World's Pain* a work of prophecy? It wasn't possible, surely! How could a book silently impose itself on the real world? And yet it would seem that this was precisely what was happening, for as he turned the page to continue, a small rectangle of newsprint, a bookmark, fell out and fluttered to the floor. Jeremy reached down to pick it up and as he turned it over he was horrified and reassured in almost equal measure to see that familiar fedora and burnt-tissue grin.

But wait!

Had the spelling changed, or had he simply misremembered?

K-R-U-*E*?

He tore a strip of masking tape from the roll around his wrist and stuck the picture of Freddie Krueger to the wall next to the blurry black and white photo of Chernobyl, then continued reading.

Thursday May 1 1986

The incident with the pigeon at the traffic lights[103] meant that after her English seminar Laura had spent the rest of the day stuck in the casualty department of the LGI with a twisted ankle. Luckily Laura's mum had given her a new 200 unit BT Phonecard in her Christmas stocking. It was the same size as her cheque guarantee card so she kept it in her purse for emergencies, in case she ever needed to make a call when she was out, but didn't have 10p on her. The phone on the landing outside their flat on St John's Terrace was for outgoing, paid calls only, you couldn't dial in, so she hadn't been able to ring Jeremy and let him know. Instead, Laura had rung her friend Liz who lived down in the Harolds and had a clapped out old mini, and asked if she might be able to come and give her a lift home.

It had been gone 8 o'clock when she got back to the flat, hobbling up to the first floor one step at a time with her walking stick, by which time Jeremy had been in full angry young man[104] 'mode', his hands metallic-grey from the raw graphite drawing stick that she was horrified to see he'd been using to annotate and draw over and around various newspaper cuttings that were hanging[105] from the wall behind the sofa. He was listening to *Combat Rock*. The track entitled 'Overpowered by Funk[106]'. What looked like the remainder[107] of the newspapers were loosely screwed up and strewn across the floor, as if he'd been going through them, page by page, day by day[108]; keeping this, discarding that. It was with some dismay that Laura wondered if this might turn into an endless task, like painting the Forth[109] Bridge. She hadn't dared go[110] in and look more closely and so, unwilling to either flatter or to challenge the artistic ego, let alone to raise the small matter[111] of their deposit and be seen unjustly as the nag[112] in all of this, she'd retreated and made herself a kiwi[113] fruit sandwich and a glass of water in their tiny stand-up kitchen, then taken a codeine painkiller and with some difficulty gone to bed for a fitful night of swamp dreams in which she'd journeyed with a ferryman[114] through Niger[115] waterways

---

[103]   1 across: 'Signals with three colours (7, 6).' Quick Crossword 5,007. *The Guardian*, 1 May 1986
[104]   2 down: 'Anti-establishment writer etc (5, 5, 3).' #5,007. *Ibid.*
[105]   22 across: 'Deed liable to capital punishment? (7, 6).' (first part.) #5,007. *Ibid.*
[106]   16 across: 'Fear, often blue (4).' #5,007. *Ibid.*
[107]   20 across: 'Residue (9).' #5,007. *Ibid.*
[108]   10 across: 'As time goes on (3, 2, 3).' #5,007. *Ibid.*
[109]   13 down: 'Do not abide at home (2, 5).' (second part.) #5,007. *Ibid.*
[110]   13 down: 'Do not abide at home (2, 5).' (first part.) #5,007. *Ibid.*
[111]   22 across: 'Deed liable to capital punishment? (7, 6).' (second part.) #5,007. *Ibid.*
[112]   21 across: 'Horse – henpeck! (3).' #5,007. *Ibid.*
[113]   19 down: 'New Zealand bird (4).' #5,007. *Ibid.*
[114]   3 down: 'He takes passengers over water (8).' #5,007. *Ibid.*
[115]   18 down: 'African country and river (5).' #5,007. *Ibid.*

overhung with wistaria[116] and infested with alligator and cayman[117].

When Laura awoke late to the realisation that she didn't actually own the tiny, golden-haired lap-dog[118] of her dreams, she was momentarily disappointed. She could hear the sound of morning break at the Grammar School over the way, a ball being kicked, and in one of those sudden swoops of the imagination she saw the thousands of other games of football that were being played simultaneously in all the school playgrounds of Europe.

Or most of them. She also imagined empty playgrounds: Soviet schools, drab and deserted in evacuated towns.

Needing air she reached over and opened the curtain to what was a beautiful Mayday morning. The sash was open a notch and a light breeze still carried the lingering coolness of night time, and with it the delicate rustling of the bright green horse-chestnut[119] leaves in next door's garden.

There were no lectures today, but she'd a load of things to do. Not least of which was to go to Liz's and call her brother to see if there was any news from her parents in Turkey. However, the way her ankle was feeling Laura didn't think she'd even make it down the ten steps to the pay-phone on the landing, so she lay there, wishing they had a radio, pondering her own immobility and thinking about her parents. Presumably they were wandering around oblivious to the global[120] event that was unfolding on the other side of the Black Sea. Her father hunting out dog-eared postcards in junk shops before lunch, or those little cellophane packets of old stamps. Acutely aware of her own powerlessness, Laura realised that she couldn't even write to them.

She also wondered whether Jeremy had got any sleep; the state he'd been in last night.

A short while later she heard a familiar tread on the path, followed by front door rattle and the squeak of staircase linoleum. Jeremy poked his head around the bedroom door and stood there, half-in, half-out. She was relieved to see that he'd washed at least. Got most of it off.

'Pinch punch,' he said, only slightly hauntedly. Then, 'How's the foot?'

'Ankle, really. So swollen,' said Laura, who had resigned herself to an idle[121] day. 'I can't move. Anything to eat?'

'Yeah!' he said, lifting up the carrier bag he was holding in his left hand. 'From t' stale bread shop.' This was their name for the grocers on the corner of Harold View – down behind the Royal[122] Park – which sold day-old, crusty white

---

116	12 down: 'It was air (anag) – shrub (8).' #5,007. *Ibid.*
117	4 down: 'Type of alligator (6).' #5,007. *Ibid.*
118	15 down: 'Pampered pet (3-3).' #5,007. *Ibid.*
119	6 down: 'Conker tree (5-8).' #5,007. *Ibid.*
120	13 across: 'Referring to the whole world (6).' #5,007. *Ibid.*
121	5 down: 'Lazy or vain (4).' #5,007. *Ibid.*
122	9 across: 'London hospital (5, 4).' (first part.) #5,007. *Ibid.*

bread for 5p. 'Toast and Marmite? Boiled egg[123]?'

'Can you get me my painkillers too?' she asked.

'What's the magic word?'

'*Now!*'

'Look,' he lifted up another carrier bag that he'd been hiding behind the door and transferred that to his left hand too, then reached in and took out a 7" single. 'From the Welton Road Community Shop! Where I got the Slim Smith record that time. Hang on...'

Seconds later she heard the speaker[124] in the living room crackle with the sound of stylus on vinyl, before – unexpectedly – the familiar zither[125] sounds of the theme from *The Third Man*.

'Anton Karas,' shouted Jeremy. 'On London Records. From 1950!'

When he reappeared he was wearing a not-too-bad tweed[126] jacket over his combats. 'Two quid,' he said, modelling it stiff-armedly. 'And he gave me the record for free[127]!'

Laura dozed of after her tea and toast. Maybe it was the painkillers. She awoke to hear Jeremy swearing. Her heart sank as she raised her voice just enough to be heard in the next room: 'What is it?'

When he came in to answer he was holding the newspaper: 'It's all connected, Lor.'

'What is?'

'All of it. I think it's something to do with the graphite,' he said, more matter-of-factly than this cryptic assertion might have allowed. 'I don't know. *The Guardian*, Chernobyl, the zone of death, us, me, you, everything.'

'What do you mean?' Laura asked, worriedly.

'Well, it's Thursday, and look at the book page in today's paper,' he said, walking over and handing her the folded broadsheet. 'I couldn't believe it.'

Laura's eye was drawn first to a paperback ad running down column one, which announced, 'four exciting new titles by writers with style, wit and narrative drive,' including Thomas M. Disch and that lugubrious Jonathan Meades bloke off the telly, but also – far more exciting to Laura, who had been thinking of doing her dissertation on her – Kathy Acker's *Don Quixote*.

'Wow! *Don Quixote*. Great!' Sensing her boyfriend's impatience, she then looked to where Jeremy was actually pointing. It took a while with the small print, but the second of the three reviews on that week's *Guardian* book page included a new Michael Moorcock novel: *The City in the Autumn Stars*.

---

[123]   8 across: 'Object of laying (3).' #5,007. *Ibid.*

[124]   7 down: 'Official of the House of Commons (7).' #5,007. *Ibid.*

[125]   14 across: 'Stringed instrument (6).' #5,007. *Ibid.*

[126]   1 down: 'River – cloth (5).' #5,007. *Ibid.*

[127]   9 across: 'London hospital (5, 4).' (second part.) #5,007. *Ibid.*

'More and Moorcock!' she flirted, pointlessly.

'Yes, but...' After a few seconds' pause he added: 'It's another Von Bek!'

'Von what? I'm a bit spaced out,' said Laura, shaking her head as if that might help her understand. 'These painkillers. You're not trashing the place are you Jeremy? We do need your month's deposit back. I do. You said it was a loan, remember? It was a hundred and something pounds.'

'You know yesterday,' said Jeremy, ignoring her, 'when I read you that bit of Moorcock and it was like a description of the radiation zone around Chernobyl?'

'Yes,' she said, 'kind of a coincidence at least. I can see that. What of it?'

'That Von Bek – *The Warhound and the World's Pain* – was published in 1981, and *this*,' he pointed at the review excitedly, as if it explained everything, 'is a new sequel to that book! *In today's paper*! Another Von Bek *out this week*! Look at the timing! Do you think *that's* a coincidence?'

'Are you going to go and buy it?' Laura asked, struggling to understand. 'Going to go to Austicks and buy it?'

'No way!' said Jeremy. 'Spend nearly half my giro? Are you kidding? No, I'll see if the library are going to order it! But anyway, listen to what the reviewer says. Um, "not to be despised..." That's so snobby and partisan[128], and yet so passive! "Not to be despised,"' he put on a comedy-supercilious voice, '"*even by those with no particular yen for what I believe is called swords and sorcery.*"[xvii] What does it even mean? I *hate* double-negatives! Who does he think he is? What a jerk[129]!'

Laura, effectively trapped, shook her head.

'Anyway,' said Jeremy, really babbling now, 'if the first book of Von Bek is a work of prophecy about what is happening right now, then if this is coming out now, too, it must also be, I don't know,' and here Jeremy's amphetamine logic, stoned and circular, threatened to spiral vertiginously down some psychic plughole, 'it must also be prophesying *itself*.'

Friday May 2 1986

'Listen,' Laura said. 'What kind of bird is that?'

'Herald[130] of the dawn!' said Jeremy, credulous[131] as only the sleeping can be. 'The blackbird[132] is actually a type of thrush[133].'

Class[134] dismissed, she had thought as he turned back over. She marvelled

---

[128]   17 across: 'Biassed – guerilla! (8).' #5,007. *Ibid.*
[129]   11 across: 'Sudden pull (4).' #5,007. *Ibid.*
[130]   15 across: 'Announcer (6).' Quick Crossword 5,008. *The Guardian*, 2 May 1986
[131]   12 down: 'Prepared to believe anything (9).' #5,008. *Ibid.*
[132]   9 across: 'Relative of 18 down (9).' #5,008. *Ibid.*
[133]   18 down: 'Bird, song or missel (6).' #5,008. *Ibid.*
[134]   13 down: 'Excellence – at school? (5).' #5,008. *Ibid.*

at his seamless resumption of sensibleness and wondered if she should give him the chop[135] now that she could. Was it just that? Or were what she had once thought of as 'his artistic ways' in fact nothing more than a product of recreational drug use? Ranting wretch[136] one minute, pompous know-it-all the next. It had to stop[137]. After Wednesday night and cast uncomfortably once again in the role[138] of mother, hoping he wouldn't play up[139], she had come close to imposing a curfew[140] on the chump[141], but he – of sleepless pallor[142] and dead on his restless feet – had gone to bed before the *Nine O' Clock News* had even finished.

Laura couldn't get back to sleep though. It wasn't her ankle or the blackbird but some deeper itch[143] that was keeping her awake: her parents in Turkey. She hoped they were safe. She thought of her mother in that funny nylon tabard[144] housecoat thing, baking a flan[145]; her father's philately[146]. It was as if summoning their cartoon versions might cast some protective aura around the real them. What else could she do, short[147] of going out there herself and putting them on a plane.

On other nights like this she had sat up in their modest[148] bedroom trying to summon such an image of herself and Jeremy in twenty-odd years' time, but hadn't been able to do it.

Perhaps that had been a good thing after all; a reprieve.

Three thousand victims, an article in yesterday's paper had said, based on US intelligence: an epidemic of cancers and birth defects. 'Other consequences'[xviii] playing out for decades. There was a map showing that the cloud had changed direction and would reach northern Italy by noon on Saturday. Pictures of the building had been shown on Soviet TV. Apparently it was no longer billowing smoke. Duty calls[149], she thought, but for whom? Who was putting out the fire, who going close enough to take the pictures? Men, roused from lover's bed or barrack but returning to a condemned cell[150]? Were they able to actually feel the radiation as they stared into that great, broken shell[151]? How was it possible to even thank them? Some

---

135   11 down: 'Piece of meat (for a fool?) (5, 4).' (second part.) #5,008. *Ibid.*

136   16 across: 'Miserable person (6).' #5,008. *Ibid.*

137   7 down: 'Don't go all the way (4, 5).' (first part.) #5,008. *Ibid.*

138   2 down: 'Part (4).' #5,008. *Ibid.*

139   19 down: 'Do your best or be a nuisance (4, 2).' #5,008. *Ibid.*

140   5 down: 'Evening bell, clearing the streets (6).' #5,008. *Ibid.*

141   11 down: 'Piece of meat (for a fool?) (5, 4).' (first part.) #5,008. *Ibid.*

142   19 across: 'Wanness (6).' #5,008. *Ibid.*

143   3 down: 'Craving (4).' #5,008. *Ibid.*

144   4 down: '15 across's coat (thanks, poet!) (6).' #5,008. *Ibid.*

145   23 down: 'Open tart or sponge (4).' #5,008. *Ibid.*

146   6 down: 'Stamp collecting (9).' #5,008. *Ibid.*

147   7 down: 'Don't go all the way (4, 5).' (second part.) #5,008. *Ibid.*

148   17 across: 'Unassuming (6).' #5,008. *Ibid.*

149   24 across: 'I must go and do some work (4, 5).' #5,008. *Ibid.*

150   21 across: 'Small room (4).' #5,008. *Ibid.*

151   20 across: 'Outer casing (5).' #5,008. *Ibid.*

sort of global whip-round[152]? This was not, she thought, the shot[153] heard around the world. It was more like a clap[154] of thunder that would just keep rumbling on; death toll ever rising. And as it did so, would the anniversary come to be marked like some atomic Armistice[155] Day? Everyone stopping work for a minute's silence? Bowed heads around the world, from creek[156] to kraal[157]?

Birth defects.

She remembered that winter morning back in the new year. Waking up with something like period pain but much, much worse. Jeremy's hesitant touch on her shoulder while she was sick; puke like sago[158] pudding. Blood. Then him hopping out barefoot on to the freezing landing linoleum to call an ambulance.

On the way to the hospital, with a green woollen blanket tucked across her lap and a rubber cuff being velcroed and inflated around her bicep, she had been suddenly and unexpectedly struck with the shame of it. She could remember thinking that it was lucky she hadn't told many people.

A blighted ovum[159], the doctor had said later, with rehearsed concern, then, more brightly: 'It happens! You should try again.'

Saturday May 3 1986

Without ever really looking at it, Laura had always simply assumed that the man pictured on the banknote that was stuck on their fridge door was Yul Brynner, but now she came to think of it why would the French be offering this normally posthumous and nationalistic honour to the star of *The King and I*? Yes, he was dead *now*, but only just. Looking at it this closely, Laura could see the cross-hatched shading on his face and – for the first time – that he was quite clearly labelled otherwise, although what the actual silk-turbaned one's claim to such eternal[160] numismatic life might be she didn't know. Also, was it a turban, or something else? The phrase *da capo*[161] came to mind. Did that mean something to do with the head or an actual cap? Her ignorance of French history was understandable though, surely, and wouldn't a French person faced with Isaac Newton on a pound note, or the Duke of Wellington on a fiver be similarly stumped?

Actually, no, she thought. No, they wouldn't.

---

152   26 across: 'Appeal for money for present etc. (4-5).' #5,008. *Ibid.*
153   8 across: 'Hit with gun (4).' #5,008. *Ibid.*
154   10 across: 'Applaud (4).' #5,008. *Ibid.*
155   1 across: 'Truce (9).' #5,008. *Ibid.*
156   13 across: 'Arm of river (5).' #5,008. *Ibid.*
157   14 down: 'Village of huts (5).' #5,008. *Ibid.*
158   22 down: 'Milk pudding (4).' #5,008. *Ibid.*
159   25 across: 'Egg (4).' #5,008. *Ibid.*
160   24 across: 'Everlasting (7).' Quick Crossword 5,009. *The Guardian*, 3 May 1986
161   15 down: 'Start again (in music) (2, 4).' #5,009. *Ibid.*

It had been a present from someone. Perhaps an ex-girlfriend of Jeremy's or more likely a *not-quite*-girlfriend, some crush for whom he unwittingly functioned as a kind of token[162] boy. She had been to Paris, this friend of his whatever her name was, and brought it back for him, and due to whatever probably unwarranted loyalty he had stuck it on the fridge the day they'd moved in here, or – strictly speaking – the day he had moved in. Yes, she had covered the deposit from her savings, and yes, she had slept here just as many nights as him, but no, her name wasn't on the rent book or the tenancy agreement, and officially – as far as the dole were concerned anyway – she didn't exist. They even kept a sleeping bag and pillow rolled up down the side of the sofa, with a ruck sack containing some of her clothes and a dummy wash-bag complete with tampons. All of this in the not altogether completely paranoid anticipation of an unexpected early morning knock at the door, and the sudden need to prove to some DHSS inspector that she was indeed just a visitor, and that Jeremy deserved his single person rates. They'd heard horror stories of fascistic jobsworths, seemingly trained to distrust doleys and hate students, arriving unannounced at the homes of couples they knew and snooping around, asking trick questions to try and prove that you were cohabiting. As if it was any of their business! As if it was any skin off their nose! Laura shuddered at the prospect, then remembered from her piano lessons that *da capo* was a musical term, an instruction meaning repeat from the beginning.

Jeremy – who had not yet sufficiently apologised for the vast and messy, newspaper and graphite, collaged wall drawing next door – was listening to *Smile Jamaica*, a free ska and reggae compilation given away on the cover of the NME. It was her cassette, but had become one of their favourites: 'It's like *Creation Rockers* volume seven!' Jeremy had said for the umpteenth time as he lit up yet another Saturday afternoon spliff that upon reflection she realised had been far too strongly packed. Right now she could hear the familiar ska shuffle of 'Solomon[163] Gundie' and what was it that she was meant to be doing? Why was she leaning on the fridge door looking at an engraving of Maurice Quentin de la Tour?

'Ten across,' he'd said as she got up to leave the room. 'That's easy: May-tree[164]. Hey Lor, did you know that Hawthorn blossom is used in Mayday celebrations because it smells of death?'

'*No*,' she'd said, pulling a face. 'Obviously not.'

'I love the smell. This is my favourite time of year!' he added. 'Maybe that's because I was born in May.'

'Hint, hint,' she'd chided. But now, victim of a sudden head rush and leaning against the fridge, one thing she did know was that the elaborate and asymmetrical scrolled device next to de la Tour's portrait on the French fifty franc[165]

---

162   19 down: 'Symbol (5).' #5,009. *Ibid.*
163   1 across: 'Type of the wise (7).' #5,009. *Ibid.*
164   10 across: 'Hawthorn (3-4).' #5,009. *Ibid.*
165   11 across: 'Foreign currency (5).' #5,009. *Ibid.*

note was a Rococo cartouche, and come to think of it she'd never even questioned what it was that this kind of ultra-ornamental but empty picture frame might have to do with the star of *West World*. However, she knew that it was a cartouche because Jeremy had had to explain the Rococo to her once.

Laura still went hot and blotchy to remember how back in the early days of their relationship, perhaps the first time he'd come back to her old room in Victoria Road, no they would have been in Jeremy's Brudenell basement, and he was in the middle of some art-historical *spiel* or other and had mentioned a particular kind of Rococo artefact, to which her guileless response had been, 'Rococo? What colour is that?'

'Laura[166] Morris[167]!' Jeremy had spluttered, taking *The Story of Art* from his book shelf. 'Shame on you! Interest in literature does not preclude a knowledge of art history!'

Their knees had touched as he'd sat down next to her on the bed and opened the book to begin half-seriously explaining something or other about the Rococo – anti-architectural this, shell-like that – but she couldn't quite remember what it was because their knees were touching and it hadn't taken long before Ernst Gombrich was lying face-down on the carpet and they were continuing the lesson in Jeremy's single bed, him drawing asymmetrical and oh so ornamental scrolls on the skin of her back as they lay beneath the new continental quilt that he'd been telling her about when they met for the first time in the back room of the Royal[168] Park pub earlier that evening via his friend Rosy[169] who was a friend of a friend of Siân's or Nicky's.

They had been going out together pretty much ever since, moving in together – or not – last September. Thinking about his enthusiasm it just wasn't fair, him getting turned down by the Fine Art course like that. Of course that was why he was a bit more fragile than usual, wandering around like some dyspeptic[170] conspiracy theorist and smoking far too much dope. He sometimes got what Laura thought of as real stoner's eyes – red, puffy and glassy-lensed – and would sit there, blinking slowly like a turtle[171]. In face of such behaviour and let off the hook of early pregnancy, Laura had stopped wondering if she and Jeremy would stay the course[172]. Perhaps it was simply a matter of self-preservation, but her devastation about the miscarriage had been transformed into a sense of relief. Maybe the truth of it was that ill-chosen[173], they had no real future after all because they didn't share enough in common to sustain a relationship which as a result had been less rent asunder[174] than

---

[166]   2 down: 'Girl's name (from shrub) (5).' #5,009. *Ibid.*
[167]   6 down: 'Old English dance (6).' #5,009. *Ibid.*
[168]   20 down: 'R. (5).' #5,009. *Ibid.*
[169]   12 down: 'Pink and optimistic? (4).' #5,009. *Ibid.*
[170]   15 across: 'Bad-tempered from indigestion (9).' #5,009. *Ibid.*
[171]   17 down: 'Chelonian or dove (6).' #5,009. *Ibid.*
[172]   5 down: 'Persevere to the end (4, 3, 6).' #5,009. *Ibid.*
[173]   13 across: 'Unlike the expert's "few words"? (3, 6).' #5,009. *Ibid.*
[174]   9 across: 'Apart (as below!) (7).' #5,009. *Ibid.*

simply outworn[175], but how in his present state would he take another knock-back?

Laura pushed the horrible thoughts to the back of her mind and took the eggs out of the fridge. She was meant to be making a snack: scrambled because omelettes set off the smoke alarm in their inadequately ventilated kitchenette. There wasn't time to discuss their future or lack of it right now, because she had to go and start work at six o'clock. The student shift. Saturday nights used to mean snuggling up to watch *Hill Street Blues*, maybe going out for a few pints if they had a spare fiver, or going to a gig, and they'd seen some great ones, but that was before she joined the staff[176] at the Playhouse. Now Fridays and Saturdays meant serving the pre-theatre or pre-screening drinks, and taking interval orders, fulfilling them during the first act and waiting for the onslaught that came with the intermission. Luckily the bar closed during the second act on a theatre night, but still it took ages to clear up and they were lucky to finish by a quarter to eleven. The perks were that if it wasn't sold out she could generally sneak in and catch some or most of a late screening, although it was the full-timers on ticket duty who had the best of it, and got to see the whole play or film for free.

She would rather that she didn't have to go out at all to be quite honest, because according to *The Guardian* the radiation cloud had now reached Britain. At work on Friday night, CND Steve had said that the gossip in anti-nuclear circles was that in the event of this happening, top secret civil defence measures were ready to be brought into play: plans that had been developed for nuclear war rather than civil nuclear disaster.

'Such as?' she'd asked. 'You mean tanks on the streets and calming speeches on the telly to put people at their ease[177]?'

'Skateboarding ducks, more like,' Steve had said. 'Or a cuddly, otter[178] documentary, while they round up the dissidents. Some traffic-warden-come-turnkey[179]-type on every left-wing journalist's doorstep at dawn. Don't you read the *Leeds Other Paper*?' Then he'd added that the least the government could do would be to issue everyone with sodium iodide tablets, which had made Laura think of childhood bicycle accidents and scraped knees; yellow disinfectant and stitches. Steve said that the iodine in the tablets could help prevent thyroid cancer, although the government would probably feel that to take such precautionary measures, or to give people real or useful information would spread panic, and not just about Chernobyl but about nuclear power generally.

Steve's opinion was that they'd rather keep us all badly-informed regardless of the consequences! 'Telling us,' he said, 'that it's not safe to drink rainwater one minute, but that it's okay to eat the meat or drink the milk of animals

---

[175]   8 across: 'Shibboleths usually are (7).' #5,009. *Ibid.*
[176]   1 down: 'Body of administrators (5).' #5,009. *Ibid.*
[177]   14 down: 'Leisure or simplicity (4).' #5,009. *Ibid.*
[178]   18 across: 'Water animal (5).' #5,009. *Ibid.*
[179]   22 across: 'Gaoler (7).' #5,009. *Ibid.*

who *eat* the grass that's been rained on the next! What they don't tell you is that this kind of radiation gradually builds up in the food chain and concentrates in your bones or your lungs or whatever.'

'Blimey,' said Laura.

'Check out the *LOP* next Friday,' he'd added conspiratorially. 'I hear from a very reliable source that they're going to be covering it properly: a double-page spread of radiation information.'

They had been interrupted by the interval rush, Laura still limping slightly and needing to rest on a bar stool in between customers, but her ankle felt much better after the best part of two days in bed. A 'very reliable source' indeed! What Steve had meant, thought Laura, was that he'd had a pint in the Fenton with Dave who helped out in Cookridge Street a couple of days a week!

And now here it was: the cloud. The paper said that by this morning south-easterly winds would have carried the fallout over most of the country, and there was no sign yet of any 'Protect and Survive'-type action here in Leeds 6. There were no loudspeakers in the streets, no army ambulances dispensing urgent medicines on street corners, and no air-raid sirens. Laura had checked to see if there was any iodine in the medicine chest[180] on the wall of their shared bathroom, which surprise-surprise there wasn't. Would a parasol[181] be effective protection against radiation? She imagined a sort of Heath Robinson contraption. A fallout catcher[182] made of bellows and brollies, with mechanical dustpans and brushes mounted on a lead hat.

A government spokesman was reported as saying that there was no risk to the public. It was almost beyond satire[183] the way they were talking about background levels and whatnot. You'd think it was normal[184], that radiation was safe! And they were all saying that the Russians were being secretive! Laura had seen *The War Game* when she was in the fifth year doing O-levels. Guildford CND had organised a minibus to go and watch a screening of a 16mm print in a room above a pub in the nearby town of Farnham, so she was no stranger to the gist of Steve's conversation. As far as she was concerned, it was to be expected that establishment voices would deny any danger. Yet apparently there was some local Moscow apparatchik in Germany telling reporters that lead and sand was being dropped from helicopters onto the reactor to try and stop the radiation; that it could kill a child in one hour, an adult in four. Pity the poor chopper pilots then, she'd thought. This Yeltsin character told West German TV reporters that towns had been evacuated, water contaminated. Christ, was he mad? Certainly he was either very brave or very stupid, and she half-expected to read that he'd immediately either

---

180   3 down: 'Drug container (8, 5).' #5,009. *Ibid.*
181   23 across: 'Sunshade (7).' #5,009. *Ibid.*
182   21 across: 'Baseball player (in the rye?) (7).' #5,009. *Ibid.*
183   16 down: 'Serious humour (6).' #5,009. *Ibid.*
184   4 down: 'Customary (6).' #5,009. *Ibid.*

defected or been disappeared. Perhaps the Soviet authorities would intern[185] him when he returned to Moscow.

Here in Britain, it was perfectly safe. If the Orwellian-sounding National Radiological Protection Board were to be believed. According to them, danger levels would only occur where the radiation was 'concentrated by rainfall.'

'Oh, phew! What a relief!' she had said in an exaggeratedly cheerful voice, remembering the conversation with Steve and handing the paper back to Jeremy so that he could continue doing the crossword while she made the scrambled eggs on toast. 'Well, that's okay then! Because it doesn't bloody rain much here, does it!'

Monday May 5 1986

Laura's friend Liz had suggested a Bank Holiday day out and Laura hadn't needed to be asked twice. It was a shame all the shops were closed because normally they might have had a stroll around what had become their own particular circuit of Leeds city centre. Chatting while they walked, they might pop into Schofield's to buy make-up, or Chelsea Girl to see what new clothes had come in. Laura had an account with the Alliance and Leicester Building Society which was also on Albion Street, and on these days out she would take the book with her in her handbag just in case they found something she liked, so that she could go and take some money out if she needed to.

They would walk down to Boar Lane stopping to look at all the musical instruments and random electronic tat in the windows of We Buy Owt, then the various herbs and tinctures, and the essential oil burners that were displayed in The Sorcerer's Apprentice. They would usually take the long way back around to the Headrow via the covered market and the various arcades, finally perhaps stopping in at Morrisons in the Merrion Centre on the way home if they needed anything, or going and borrowing a record from the World Music section in the library, before catching a number 56 bus home.

On a sunny day like this they might have taken a bus out to Otley and sat by the weir in the sun, but what with her ankle and everything the prospect of a picnic on the moors didn't really appeal, and that was without the sudden likelihood of radioactive grass or sheep. Laura didn't fancy going to the cinema either, even if it meant for once being able to see a whole, non-art-house film, voting[186] instead to go back to Liz's down in the Harolds.

The two friends had arrived in Leeds at the same time, nearly two years before. They were on different courses, Liz doing sociology to Laura's English, but they'd both ended up in the same shared house on Victoria Road in their first years – way down by the Norwoods at the Cardigan Road end – and although Liz could

185   7 down: 'Oblige to live within limits (6).' #5,009. *Ibid.*
186   14 across: 'Exercising franchise (6).' Quick Crossword 5,010. *The Guardian*, 5 May 1986

sometimes be outspoken[187], Laura had come to rely on her staunch friendship and support[188], just as Liz had come to think of Laura as her best friend.

Liz tootled up in the car, beeping the horn and waiting outside rather than coming in as she might otherwise do, for a cup of mint tea or something, and when Laura went downstairs to meet her she was surprised to see a postcard from Turkey propped up on the shelf in the hall. One of the neighbours must have taken it in with their own post on Saturday by mistake, because it hadn't been there on Sunday and there had been no delivery this Bank Holiday morning. The card was, as she hoped, from her parents on their package deal[189] in 'Lasagna[190]-on-sea[191]' as Jeremy seemed to delight in calling any European holiday destination. The picture on the card was of a bar[192] overlooking a beautiful lagoon[193] at a place called Ölüdeniz on the Mediterranean coast. Turning it over, she read it as she walked down the long garden path. 'Our own[194] dear Laura,' it said:

> Coach journeys uneventful. Lovely few days up on the Black Sea coast in Trabzon (Byzantine churches etc), where (honestly) they believe that oak[195] trees don't worship God – & they're prob. right! We spent a day in Sardis where Aesop[196] lived (D got you fab tea towel!) but now on the Med and back in 20th century. Thinking of you & Love to J. Lots of love M+D

'Have a great[197] time!' said Jeremy, after declining an ambiguous[198] offer to join Laura and Liz that he could tell was only made out of something like politeness. He was having one of what his girlfriend called his 'tortured artist' days, and had put Moorcock's *The Warhound and the World's Pain* to one side for the moment. Scanning the book shelf he had briefly considered the pulpy New English Library delights of Hugh Miller's *Kingpin*[199] ('Behind the glamour of the pop business is a sleazy world of easy exchange'), but ended up plumping for his well-thumbed paperback of *The Snow Goose*[200]. It was that kind of day. To complete the experience he was also listening to *A Live Album* by the rock band Camel, not because some of

---

187   12 down: 'Frank (9).' #5,010. *Ibid.*
188   18 across: 'Back(ing) (7).' #5,010. *Ibid.*
189   1 across: 'Transaction taking the rough with the smooth? (7, 4).' #5,010. *Ibid.*
190   13 across: 'Type of pasta (7).' #5,010. *Ibid.*
191   19 down: 'Like Southend etc (2, 3).' #5,010. *Ibid.*
192   10 across: 'Where lawyers drink? (3).' #5,010. *Ibid.*
193   15 across: 'Enclosed piece of sea (6).' #5,010. *Ibid.*
194   23 down: 'Possess' (3).' #5,010. *Ibid.*
195   21 across: 'Tree (3).' #5,010. *Ibid.*
196   20 across: 'Fabulous writer! (5).' #5,010. *Ibid.*
197   8 down: 'Relative (5-6).' (first part.) #5,010. *Ibid.*
198   6 down: 'Of uncertain meaning (9).' #5,010. *Ibid.*
199   3 down: 'Principal person or bolt (7).' #5,010. *Ibid.*
200   22 across: 'Arctic bird (4, 5).' #5,010. *Ibid.*

it had been recorded in Leeds, although it had, but because it featured a song cycle that was based on the novella.

Laura couldn't bear either the record or the book. '*Black Beauty* for boys,' she'd say, and whenever Jeremy put the record on she would jokingly call it 'The Slow Noose', detesting its hideous and ponderous amalgam[201] of prog-rock and orchestral boogie. Jeremy didn't mind Laura's disdain because after all *she* liked Cat Stevens who was the absolute dregs[202] as far as he was concerned, so he figured they were about even. Besides which, for him *The Snow Goose* was all bound up with his childhood desire to become an artist. He'd seen Camel performing a couple of songs from their musical tribute on the *Old Grey Whistle Test* when he would have been around ten or eleven years old. It had made a big impression on him in those pre-punk years, and his parents happened to have had the book by Paul Gallico.

The novella was about a disabled artist called Phillip Rhayader who lives in a lighthouse and who rescues first the eponymous bird (which is brought to him injured by a young girl called Fritha) and then hundreds of British soldiers from the beaches of Dunkirk; a mission from which he does not return. However, the snow goose does come back for one last visit to the grown up Fritha, who has been waiting at the lighthouse for news of Phillip, whom she loves. The white bird also lives on in the stories of Dunkirk evacuation survivors, for whom the soaring form has become a sort of symbol or an angel of deliverance.

The Snow Goose contained everything that Jeremy wanted from the creative life as he approached adolescence. It had isolation, unrequited love and a kind of heroic artistic suicide. It also had nice drawings by Sir Peter Scott, and in his early teens Jeremy had eagerly and faithfully copied these, perfecting the droop[203] of the injured bird's neck or it's final triumphant flight; a rescued soldier being pulled up onto the aft[204] of Rhayader's little sailing boat in those strafed and choppy waters off Dunkirk. Some of his drawings had been turned into birthday or get well soon cards to grandparents, or to aunts and uncles from their loving nephew[205].

Jeremy would ask for art equipment for Christmas and birthday presents, and on Saturday lunchtimes he would meet his friends at The Left Bank record shop on Paris Street, where they would look through the LPs and listen to new singles, after which he might walk around to Bedford Street and browse among the putty rubbers and the watercolours in Eland's, taking home soft-leaded pencils and carefully rolled sheets of cartridge paper, and perhaps a couple of small tubes of Windsor & Newton gouache paint that from the age of about sixteen he was able to buy with the wages from his Friday evening and Saturday job, stacking shelves in the wines and spirits aisle at Key Markets. Sometimes he and his friends would go

---

[201]   16 down: 'Mixture of metals (7).' #5,010. *Ibid.*
[202]   5 down: 'Sediment of drink (5).' #5,010. *Ibid.*
[203]   11 across: 'Wilt (5).' #5,010. *Ibid.*
[204]   2 down: 'Astern (3).' #5,010. *Ibid.*
[205]   8 down: 'Relative (5, 6).' (second part.) #5,010. *Ibid.*

and sit in the Cathedral yard and compare purchases, or take turns to read the track listings and the sleeve notes on records. Later, work finished and homework done, he would gobble[206] up supper so that he could go back up to his bedroom and attend to whatever was clipped to his drawing board. He would practice drawing his own hand or from still life, and he taught himself how to use his thumb on a pencil to measure objects; calculating their relationships and proportions by eye.

Using pastels Jeremy had once made a careful enlargement[207] of his favourite picture, squaring off a photocopy of the front cover illustration – which captured the goose in noisy take-off against a distant bank of cloud – and carefully copying each subdivision[208] over into a grid that he'd ruled out on a larger sheet of soft blue paper, drawing one square at a time until he'd made up the whole. He'd carefully erased the pencil grid and then begun to build up the pastel with controlled and even strokes, tearing off the paper wrapper on some of his older crayons so that he could use them sideways-on to produce a more impressionistic cloud effect, then using a finer point or sharp edge for the detail of the bird. When it was finished he had fixed the drawing with his mother's hair spray, so the pastel wouldn't rub off or smudge. His parents had put this into the frame in which it still hung on the living room wall in his parents', now his mother's house, although it made him cringe to see it.

As a consequence of all this investment, Gallico's book and particularly this double-album – the thing at one remove – accrued a totemic or fetishistic value for Jeremy that was only ever-so-slightly arch, even as its themes became untenable[209] and its style went so far out of fashion. His contemporaries at sixth form and foundation had looked to hipper musical sources, finding their own kinds of creative sustenance in the likes of Syd Barrett or Ian Curtis. While Jeremy liked and had bought records by both of these, he had maintained a strong[210] sense of loyalty to the story of Philip Rhayader and Fritha, and he continued to find both comfort and inspiration in the book's simple sentimentality as well as in Camel's muzak noodlings.

Tuesday May 6 1986

The junction at the western end of Woodhouse Moor, of Hyde Park Road, Woodhouse Lane and Woodhouse Street with what, a mile or so onwards[211] as you travelled out of the city would become the Otley Road, was known as Hyde Park

---

206   4 down: 'Eat greedily (6).' #5,010. *Ibid.*
207   24 across: 'Growth, as of photograph? (11).' #5,010. *Ibid.*
208   7 down: 'Group that is part of another (11).' #5,010. *Ibid.*
209   9 across: 'Indefensible or fallacious (9).' #5,010. *Ibid.*
210   17 down: 'Powerful (6).' #5,010. *Ibid.*
211   14 down: '(from now) For the future (7).' Quick Crossword 5,011. *The Guardian,* 6 May 1986

Corner. This was not because of any similarity with the architectural eclat[212] of its more grandiose namesake. That central London location was well known to both Laura and Jeremy from their regular journeys home, when, along with Leicester Forest Service Station and Swiss Cottage, it was one of the various landmarks that punctuated a nearly four-hour coach trip from Wellington Street in the centre of Leeds to Victoria Coach Station in London.

Hyde Park Corner – the real one, Laura always thought – was where the National Express coaches always took that last turn down towards Victoria. Once they had disembarked at the Coach Station and waited for the driver to retrieve their luggage, and after a welcome cup of tea and a loo break, Jeremy would have to go and board another coach down to Exeter. After seeing him off, Laura would stroll the short distance to the rail terminus to catch a train to Clapham Junction where she would change for another train to Guildford in Surrey. One of her parents would usually be waiting at the station with the car, to drive back to their house in the nearby village of Chiddingfold.

Just as much of Laura's *real* Hyde Park Corner memorialised the Duke of Wellington, so his statue, green with verdigris apart from vandalised, red-gloss-painted boots, stood at the corner of Moorland and Clarendon Roads at the University end of Woodhouse Moor, a few minutes' walk from where Jeremy and Laura lived, along their route into town, and at the diagonally opposite corner of Woodhouse Moor from the Yorkshire version.

Most of the houses along Hyde Park Road itself had been built after the national hero's death, as had the terraced streets which rolled down the hill to the west, including the Brudenells and the Royal Parks. The former streets commemorated one of Leeds' most prominent mill-owning families, upon whose former lands and parks the houses had been built following their sale to repay the family's creditors, and the latter commemorated a visit by Queen Victoria to Leeds to open the new town hall in 1858, in the course of which she had visited Woodhouse Moor. It was a visit that one hundred years later was still marked, too, in the painting on the sign of the Royal Park Pub.

The future Empress of India would have been aware of the city's reputation for being built on wool, and of its role in an Imperial trade that saw raw wool shipped from Australia and New Zealand and transported by canal from Liverpool for manufacture in West Yorkshire mills, after which it was exported back to Canada or India. It was this great industry that generated the wealth in both Sterling and Rupee[213] that had been invested back into the city in the shape of its splendid town hall. It was also what had fuelled property speculations such as these on the west side of Hyde Park Road. The smarter houses nearest to the park had been built to service the city's growing middle classes, while the back-to-back terraces further down the hill towards the woollen mills of Kirkstall and Burley had been

---

212   5 down: 'Distinction (5).' #5,011. *Ibid.*
213   16 down: 'Indian currency (5).' #5,011. *Ibid.*

erected for an impoverished working class population which in the 1840s had still been prey to exploitation and neglect[214], to flood and cholera epidemic.

Just like the real Hyde Park too, Woodhouse Moor had been a popular promenade in the 19th century, a place to see and be seen, as had the pleasure gardens that now lay, strange to say, beneath Maumoniat's Continental Supermarket and Jeremy's old basement room in Brudenell Grove.

This had also been the site of the city's equivalent of Speaker's Corner. It was all a far cry from the flat cap, ferret[215]-down-the-trousers clichés of northern industrial life. Crowds would gather along Hyde Park Road to hear speakers who would orate from specially built wooden platforms. It wasn't easy[216] now to imagine the scene: people buying the *Northern Star* while a Chartist star turn[217] spoke eloquently on matters of Parliamentary Reform.

One speaker might be arguing for the principles of a co-operative movement, another of the need for an independent party representing labour, yet another might simply be battling for the attention and respect[218] of the audience. People would gather here to debate matters of socialist ethic[219] and principle, or to campaign for workers' rights. It was a radical past that still found its echo[220] in the contemporary alternative weekly the *Leeds Other Paper*, which had been founded in the nineteen- rather than the eighteen-seventies, but was still itself run along co-operative lines.

As her own parents approached their fifties, Laura – who had merely dabbled in such ideas as part of a politics elective in her first year – found such manifestations of political and social change remarkable: the idea that in general things had *not* been ever thus, and the notion in particular that such events had been playing out on these very streets only three times longer ago than it was since her parents had been born, during the childhoods perhaps of their great great, and so her great great great grandparents.

Although she had grown up in a small Surrey village that was dominated by a medieval pub and church, and characterised by beautiful half-timbered cottages that clustered around a picture postcard village green, Laura had developed no tangible sense of history until she had left home after sixth form to come and study in Leeds, and doing so had been a little like discovering the sky. When she thought about such things now, Laura felt as if she could almost reach out and touch the lives of those previous generations of her family, who seemed more real to her in this way than they did in their occasional black-garbed and spectral presences in the handful of oldest family photographs.

---

214   4 down: 'Disregard (7).' #5,011. *Ibid.*
215   12 across: 'Trained polecat (6).' #5,011. *Ibid.*
216   7 down: 'Not how the crowned head lies (4).' #5,011. *Ibid.*
217   11 down: 'Outstanding performance (4, 4).' #5,011. *Ibid.*
218   13 down: 'Regard (7).' #5,011. *Ibid.*
219   17 down: 'Moral code (5).' #5,011. *Ibid.*
220   8 across: 'Repeated sound (4).' #5,011. *Ibid.*

She found it even more remarkable that you only had to go further back by the same period twice over to find some young oblate[221] or novitiate being received into a life of prayer and labour in the nearby Kirkstall Abbey. Although it was long-ruined this was a building that had dominated not only the landscape but also the cultural, commercial and agricultural life of the area for the preceding half-millennia. Laura had been surprised to discover that at one point a century after the Dissolution of the Monasteries, the Abbey had even been owned by those very same Brudenells.

All of this had come as a sort of private revelation to Laura, and was something that she had barely yet put into words, let alone shared with Liz or Jeremy, but when they would walk along Hyde Park Road as they were doing now, or down into town past the Fenton pub and the odd little Strawberry[222] Fields Bar next door, this sensation felt to her like just another kind of travel. Not a movement through space, or across distances at so many miles per hour[223] or feet per second[224], but through time, back through the bodies, the thoughts and the sensations of preceding generations. When she was a little bit stoned, it sometimes all felt close enough that if only she had the right kind of tape recorder[225] she might be able to actually listen to the sounds of those ancestral generations.

Laura was thinking about these things now because she was also questioning how her own and her parents' and grandparents' generations would be seen by people in the future. She was thinking about a plume of fallout which for the past week had been carried across Europe by wind-speeds of so many knots[226]. She knew both from conversations with Steve and just plain general knowledge that where ever it went, the plume, or the cloud as everyone called it, was also projecting forwards in time, from generation to generation in measurable blocks, each of which could be further multiplied by a factor of two. The thirty year half-life of caesium-137 felt almost manageable, but the one-thousand-six-hundred-and-twenty year half-life of radium-236, and the twenty-four-thousand year half-life of plutonium-239 were figures that made Laura's mind boggle.

Overlooking the junction at this Hyde Park Corner was the imposing 1930s Tudorbethan, splendour of the Hyde Park Hotel, with its stone-built ground-floor and half-timbered upper storeys. The pub was named after a hotel that had stood on the spot since the 1860s, and its lounge and public bars were flung out to south-east and south-west and at right-angles to each other as if to embrace the student drinker and to funnel him or her towards the entrance in the building's central quarter-rotunda, which was indeed where Laura and Jeremy were headed.

---

[221] 14 across: 'Flat at the poles (6).' #5,011. *Ibid.*
[222] 15 across: 'Soft fruit (10).' #5,011. *Ibid.*
[223] 19, 20 across: 'Speed (5, 3, 4).' #5,011. *Ibid.*
[224] 21 across: 'Speed (4, 3, 6).' #5,011. *Ibid.*
[225] 2 down: 'Judge or pipe (8).' #5,011. *Ibid.*
[226] 3 down: 'Nautical 19, 20 across (5).' #5,011. *Ibid.*

The Hyde Park Hotel wasn't their local, that honour went to the Royal Park, or sometimes to the Fenton, but Laura was hoping that a change of scene and a bit of Dutch courage might help her to have an exploratory chat with Jeremy, to test the water at least, or maybe even to blurt out how she was feeling. It might help that it would be unlikely they'd bump into anyone they knew particularly well. Jeremy seemed fine[227] now, she thought, after his destructive episode of a few days ago. She couldn't tell if he had been speeding or having a manic episode, but the way he was babbling about that book and staying up all night to draw on the walls it had crossed her mind that he might have been tripping. Did he still have some of that extra strong windowpane acid tucked under a corner of the hall carpet? Laura hoped not, and knew for certain that she would never take another ride on that particular roller-coaster.

They might have all been thinking rather too much about the observable and predictable behaviours of radioactive ions over vast periods of time, but as they waited at the lights to cross Headingley Lane, Laura was aware that she couldn't predict how Jeremy was going to respond to what she had to say in the next half-hour or so. She had no idea how he might take her impending rejection, her refusal[228] to carry on flogging this particular dead horse. He would be broken-hearted[229], certainly, but perhaps relieved as well, notwithstanding the fact that he'd have to somehow find the hundred and thirty quid he owed her. He could stay put, too. There'd be no need to move. His rent was covered after all. Liz had said that Laura could move into the empty attic room at her place, which would be great fun.

Laura was still very fond of Jeremy, still desired him even, and she felt enormous empathy with his dreams and ambitions. It had been a terrible blow to him not getting a place at art school. Now she supposed that he was facing the prospect of another year or more on the dole, another year of that depressing fortnightly ritual, and this was assuming everything went well. It took for granted that not only would he find another course and get it together to keep his portfolio up to date, and to apply again, but that he would get in. As far as Laura could tell none of these preconditions were necessarily achievable. She had been upset a few weeks before to find last year's prospectus[230] for Sheffield City Poly and another one for Newcastle stuffed into the bin-bag when she threw out the rubbish.

As Jeremy shouldered through the pub door and then stood with arm outstretched to hold it open so that she could enter, Laura remembered with dismay that the last time they'd been to the Hyde Park was after a visit to the Halloween funfair that was held on the bit of the park known as the Cinder Moor, on the north side of Woodhouse Lane and separated by that road from the main body of the Moor.

---

227   18 down: 'Penalty – splendid! (4).' #5,011. *Ibid.*
228   6 down: 'Saying No – often first! (7).' #5,011. *Ibid.*
229   1 across: 'Crushed by grief (6-7).' #5,011. *Ibid.*
230   10 across: 'Document describing school etc. (10).' #5,011. *Ibid.*

The date had started with a gruesomely terrifying ride on a visibly rusting octopus, but then Jeremy had won first prize on the darts stall and they were in that real first flush of love and lust so the grim ride was soon forgotten in the candy floss haze and all was going glowingly well until they had decided to have a drink at the Hyde Park Hotel, for there it was that their romantic evening had turned into a uniquely unfortunate and very perplexing kind of disaster.

The passage of some eighteen months had not rendered that night any less awful, and Laura suddenly wished they had gone somewhere else, because she realised that conversation would immediately and inevitably turn to the subject of the nameless disabled flasher or worse, who trading on the benign associations of the United Nations sweatshirt he was wearing had played on their sympathies and dominated their night out so effectively that it had culminated – was that the plan all along? – in Jeremy not only having to help him to the toilet, but also to lift him out of his wheelchair and undo his fly. After this strange and unexpected act of passive-aggressive abuse Jeremy had fled back to an only initially bemused but quickly and equally horrified Laura.

'Why didn't you just sit him on the bog and leave him to do it on his own?' she had asked, incredulously.

'I don't know,' said Jeremy. 'I didn't think.'

Leaving their half-pints of beer half-drunk on the table, they had quickly put their coats back on and half-walked, half-run all the way to Laura's shared house at the other end of Victoria Road.

Back in the safety of her shared kitchen twenty-minutes later, panting and near hysterical from a strange combination of exertion and horror, and from the challenges that the experience had presented to both of their broadly anarcho-lefty-liberal tendencies and their desires to be politically sound, they had clung to one another in silence for a few minutes. Only later did they remember to decant Jeremy's prize from the knotted polythene bag it had come in into the bottom half of a Pyrex casserole dish, pending a visit to Bobat's on Brudenell Grove the next morning where Jeremy was certain he'd seen a stack of plastic goldfish[231] bowls on the shelves behind the counter.

Wednesday May 7 1986

'Look!' said Jeremy, who had heard Laura's key in the lock and was standing in the hall waving the newspaper around excitedly with a smug[232] expression on his face.

'Can I step inside[233] first, please?' Laura asked, throwing her college bag onto the floor then taking off her jacket and hanging it up next to the large and

---

[231]   9 across: 'Inhabitant of bowl? (8).' #5,011. *Ibid.*
[232]   21 across: 'Complacent (4).' Quick Crossword 5,012. *The Guardian*, 7 May 1986
[233]   17 across: 'Invitation to enter (4, 6).' #5,012. *Ibid.*

old-fashioned fridge which occupied most of the space in their hallway.

'Sure. Sorry,' said Jeremy stepping into the kitchenette and laying the paper down on the shelf-come-breakfast bar. In fact it was two papers, folded into quarters: yesterdays and todays. He stood at the sink[234] to fill the kettle: 'Tea?'

'Lovely,' said Laura.

'What kind?'

'I don't care,' said Laura, truthfully. 'I don't know: normal? But sugary[235], please, if you're making normal.'

'Yes, that would hit the spot[236],' said Jeremy, lighting one of the gas-burning hobs on the stove. 'I bought some biscuits if you fancy.'

'Oh! *'e bought 'em!*' said Laura, imitating the cockney bank robber character's punchline from the McVities Fruit Shortcake advert that they both liked, as she followed Jeremy through the beaded curtain that divided the galley from the flat's entrance hall.

The goldfish bowl was set at the other end of the kitchen-counter, on the far side of the cooker hob and close to the small sash window which looked out across a dozen or more leafy Moorland Road back gardens towards Burley. 'How's Barbara Woodhouse?' Laura asked.

'Huh?'

Laura sort-of-nodded in the direction of the window.

'Yes, fine,' said Jeremy. 'Seems to have eaten all her sprinkles. I watched her for a bit, but frankly if you've seen one circuit of the bowl, you've seen them all.'

While they waited for the kettle, she picked away at the folds on one end of the packet of digestive biscuits until she could tear it open. Breaking off a piece she lightly shook the end-of-packet crumbs onto the counter.

'What were you saying?'

'Oh Christ, yes!' said Jeremy over-enthusiastically. 'There's a mistake in the crossword!'

'Gasp[237]!' said Laura. 'Typo in *Guardian* shock! Hardly like gold dust[238] though, are they? Isn't that why people call it the *Grauniad*?' She was wondering if she could detect the same manic edge in his voice as last week and was already growing despondent at the prospect of her boyfriend spiralling out of control again. She didn't think she had the strength[239].

'I suppose so,' said Jeremy, picking up the paper again. 'But it just struck me as funny because of the "seismologist" versus "seismographer" controversy the

---

[234]   7 down: 'Descend – in the kitchen! (4).' #5,012. *Ibid.*
[235]   14 across: 'Over-sweet (6).' #5,012. *Ibid.*
[236]   19 down: 'Notice – place! (4).' #5,012. *Ibid.*
[237]   1 across: 'Catch breath (4).' #5,012. *Ibid.*
[238]   1 down: 'Precious powder (4, 4).' #5,012. *Ibid.*
[239]   13 down: 'Power (8).' #5,012. *Ibid.*

other day. Anyway it's not exactly in the crossword itself, but there *is* a genuine mistake in the answers!

'Look, yesterday. Seventeen down, "moral code[xix]", five letters. The *real* answer was "ethic", but,' he scrabbled through the newspapers, then found what he was looking for, 'in the answers *today*, they've put "ethnic"[xx]!'

They both laughed.

'It's like, I don't know, the *something-or-other* of *Guardian* typos,' suggested Jeremy. 'The epitome!'

'Ethnic! That's *brilliant*,' Laura affirmed. 'Perfect! Almost paradigmatic!'

They basked in their enjoyment of the misprint for a second or two, until Jeremy spoke: 'Good day in the library?'

'I feel a bit like Barbara, actually,' said Laura. 'Awash. You?'

Jeremy had been working since Laura left for the library at around eight o'clock that morning. By 'working' he meant of course that he had been painting. He had also been listening to classical music: Wagner, to be precise. He had been looking after a couple of multiple-disc boxed sets of Wagner records, minding them for a music-student friend of his called Susanna who had moved back down south the previous autumn. They were live recordings of two of the four operas that constituted Wagner's *Ring Cycle*: *Die Walküre* and *Das Rheingold*. The boxes had sat there untouched, until having stared at these monoliths for several months, curiosity had seen Jeremy opening one and taking a random LP out of its sleeve and placing the disc on the turntable.

Jeremy had loved what he'd heard, and after that he played them often. Somehow the sheer bombastic force of the music seemed to help him concentrate, although even after six months he could barely differentiate the music on one disc from that on another. Perhaps it was unsurprising given that the sum total of his childhood exposure to opera had come from one or two half-remembered holiday screenings of the Bugs Bunny cartoon 'What's Opera Doc' on television. This had been supplemented more recently by a particular British Airways advert, by the French film *Diva*, and (of course) by repeated viewings of the famous helicopter bombing raid sequence in *Apocalypse Now*. Perhaps it wasn't surprising then that Jeremy found that he couldn't focus on a particular note[240] or phrase, much less get a sense of any story that was playing out. Rather it was the tempo that he responded to, and the whole dramatic sprawl[241] of the music.

He still knew next to nothing about opera, but from several superficial perusings of the large square booklets that were enclosed within each boxed set, he had learned that Richard Wagner was not only the composer of the musical component of these operatic works, but that he was also, and unusually, his own librettist[242]. To Jeremy the words seemed like further undifferentiated German mush.

---

[240]   6 down: 'Minute – sound! (4).' #5,012. *Ibid.*
[241]   16 down: 'Straggling form (of town etc) (6).' #5,012. *Ibid.*
[242]   10 down: 'Writer of words for opera (10).' #5,012. *Ibid.*

So much so that the cast and soloists might just as well, like Elmer Fudd in Chuck Jones's famous *Merry Melodies* cartoon, have been singing, 'Kill the wabbit!'

'Ah,' Laura would say, whenever she heard the familiar orchestral clamour. 'The Rinse Cycle!' She told him that Wagner was considered politically unsound, that he had been Hitler's favourite composer, that his use of Norse and Germanic legend had provided the Nazis not only with some kind of visual epic building blocks, but also that it had contributed to the warped intellectual justification for their own blood-soaked Aryan fictions-come-to-life. Laura even suggested that the darkly random-seeming, satirical, genocidal glamour of that scene in *Apocalypse Now* was not so far from the truth; just a few decades out and using a more modern military technology.

'Isn't that a bit like blaming George Stephenson for The Holocaust,' Jeremy had asked, trying to get his head around what Laura was saying. 'I mean, you know. When he built the Stockton[243] to Darlington[244] railway, he couldn't have known how the technology would be used; that the tracks would lead to Auschwitz.'

'Not at all[245], no,' Laura had replied. 'I do know what you mean, but no, I don't think it is the same, because apparently Wagner actually wrote and published all these viciously antisemitic articles too.'

'Oh, I see,' Jeremy had replied, and he did.

And now, asked to sum up his day, he said, 'Oh nothing much. Painting, you know, and listening to music. Finished the Moorcock, and did the crossword at lunchtime: the usual, really.'

He poured them a mug of tea each; handed one to Laura, then pushed the bag of sugar and the teaspoon along the counter.

'I'd been trying to find a way to bring it all together,' he said. 'The Moorcock prophecies, Chernobyl, you know.'

Laura's heart sank. She could smell the paint.

'I mean, that book,' he went on. 'It really is a kind of Cold War fantasy, the armies of the dead waiting in Middle Europe, you know, but it *is* also about Chernobyl! It really is! Even though it was written five years ago! All these visions of long-deserted ghost towns. Plus, one of the two main characters is even *from* there: from a village north of Kiev, or something.'

He paused, then just in case she didn't see what he was getting at, he repeated: '*A village north of Kiev!*'

'Lor, did you see in the paper? The press conference? That it took them days to even evacuate everyone from the *town next door* to the power station? That everyone was lying to whoever it was that they reported to, all the way up the Party structures. All of them hoping to deflect attention. All of them trying to pretend that as far as they were concerned it was all under control. Amazing!'

---

243   9 across: 'Earldom of former PM... (8).' #5,012. *Ibid.*
244   11 across: '... Other end of the line (10).' #5,012. *Ibid.*
245   22 across: 'Polite disclaimer (3, 2, 3).' #5,012. *Ibid.*

He slurped some tea.

Could he ever drink tea without slurping it, she wondered.

'So I was trying to bring it all together,' he *was* ranting now, 'but then I realised that I didn't have to, because it's Thatcher!' he said, triumphantly. '*She* is what unites all of this. So I've been painting her.'

Struggling as she was to keep up, some mental association with Margaret Thatcher reminded Laura of a demonstration she had once read about, and which had happened in 1908 on Woodhouse Moor, a stone's throw from where they were standing. Tens of thousands had turned out to campaign for women's suffrage[246]. Tens of thousands. She tried to imagine what it must have felt like, being part of that throng and that movement, yet to be hampered by all those long petticoats and enormous hats.

'You know in *Wetherby*,' he said, invoking one of their favourite films, one that had been filmed in large part around here, in the Hyde Park area of Leeds. 'You know that bit where Ian Holm, or the character he's playing, I can't remember his name, where Ian Holm anyway is saying that Thatcher's whole hate campaign is some awful act of reprisal[247]. Remember?'

Laura nodded. The smell of paint was really getting up her nose and she was kicking herself for not going through with it the night before. Laura dreaded to think where this was heading, to imagine what kind of paint-strewn domestic disaster area might be waiting next door.

'I hate the way she talks,' he said. 'The way she speaks so gently and so close to the microphone[248], to create that awful imitation of intimacy with all those hideous Tories: the kind of people who would call a bungalow a 'chalet[249]'. The way she appeals to everybody's basest instincts rather than their best. I think there is a precedent though. I think that none of it is for nothing.'

Oh Christ! Laura suddenly thought to herself, had his wall drawing been embellished: encrusted with paint, gouged out of wood-chip and plaster. Had all those oddments[250] of newspaper and that thick and filthy sheen of graphite been turned into some awful mural of Thatcher, not an inch[251] of the wall left[252] un-covered? If so she could definitely wave goodbye to her deposit.

'I think David Hare is wrong,' said Jeremy. 'I think that whatever it is that is motivating Thatcher is far, far worse than some simple, human-scale act of revenge.

'I think,' he went on, 'that if you could crawl through the wreckage at Chernobyl, if you could drag yourself through the cracks and the graphite and the

---

[246] 2 down: 'The vote (8).' #5,012. *Ibid.*
[247] 20 across: 'Tit for tat (8).' #5,012. *Ibid.*
[248] 5 down: 'Amplifier (10).' #5,012. *Ibid.*
[249] 15 across: 'Swiss-style house (6).' #5,012. *Ibid.*
[250] 3 across: 'Bits and pieces (8).' #5,012. *Ibid.*
[251] 23 across: 'Short distance (4).' #5,012. *Ibid.*
[252] 8 across: 'Remaining – on one side! (4).' #5,012. *Ibid.*

rubble and the radiation and the God-knows-what, if you were able to survive all of that somehow, and if you could get close enough to really see, to look right into the heart of the beast, if you could stare directly into the actual jaws of hell, that malevolent molten core, do you know what I think you'd see?'

Laura shook her head.

'Thatcher,' said Jeremy, matter-of-factly. 'You'd see Margaret Thatcher. I think she is after our souls. I think she really *is* the Devil.'

'What?' Laura asked, calmly, just to make sure.

'Thatcher,' he replied. 'The iron[253] maiden.' He turned and took his sketch book out from the little pile of folded newspaper. 'Listen! Who is this? What is this about?'

He opened the book and located a passage that he'd copied out from somewhere: 'Blah, blah. Okay, here we go,'

> ...Free Will, of loyalty to one's own needs. Of the importance of controlling one's own destiny. Every one believed himself to be master of his fate. And they had only one yardstick, of course: material well-being. It is all that is possible when one discounts one's involvement with the rest of humanity.[xxi]

'Is it about Margaret Thatcher?' Laura asked. 'The Tories?'

'Sounds like it doesn't it?' Jeremy nodded. 'But no. It's Lucifer. It's Satan.' He paused to let that sink in. 'It's Lucifer talking to Von Bek in *The Warhound and the World's Pain*, but it could be about Thatcher. You could almost imagine her saying something like that.'

Isn't it more interesting, Laura thought, to note the ironic distance operating in that statement? To consider Moorcock's possible suggestion that Thatcher be positioned somewhere to the right of Satan himself? But she didn't say anything. What would be the point?

Jeremy ruminated then continued: 'No, that's not quite what I mean. What I mean is that this *is* a work of prophecy, that Moorcock *was* tuning in to something bigger.

'What I mean is that if I'm right, she is going to say something like that. At some point, maybe tomorrow, maybe next year, she *will* make exactly that kind of argument: that the only measure is material, that we are all individuals and out for ourselves. That we should all, what does he say? "...discount [our] involvement with the rest of humanity."[xxii]

'And the really terrifying thing, Lor,' Jeremy was ashen-faced, 'is that people will believe her. But if they do they will be damned. She will have their souls. *That's* what she wants! Nothing less!'

---

[253]   18 down: 'Metal (4).' #5,012. *Ibid.*

'And she'll go on into her dotage[254],' he added as a kind of afterthought, 'somehow feeding off this foul harvest.'

Laura remembered the protest chant. Milk snatcher, she thought, soul catcher, and then wondered if she had Jeremy's mum's number in Exeter. Maybe she should give her a ring and see if he could go home for a bit, if there was someone who might come and pick him up. What she said, though, as brightly as she could muster, was: 'Can I see?'

Inside she was asking herself why she couldn't just go out with a plain man[255], instead of the mad artistic types that she always seemed to end up with and who cost her so much, but instead of leaving she put her mug down on the side and calmly walked through to the living room.

What Laura saw when she got there surprised her.

Jeremy had pulled the sofa out and away from the wall. There was newspaper spread out on the floor along the skirting board and a yellow car-cleaning sponge floated in a bucket of black water. The wall was almost clean, and she could see that he must have gone through several changes of water, each time moving around less and less graphite, so that now there was just a kind of uniform smear of grey that was spread evenly across the whole surface of the wall.

'Soon as it's dry I'll be able to paint over it,' said Jeremy, who had followed her in. 'There's half a tin of magnolia and some rollers under the sink.' He smiled weakly: 'Don't want to lose you your deposit.'

Every other surface in the large first floor room – the dining table, the carpet, the coffee table, the chest of drawers – was covered in large sheets of cartridge paper, each of which seemed to have a page of *The Guardian* stuck to it, to provide a ground that was then drawn over.

'Have you done all this today?' she asked.

Jeremy nodded.

'Only about thirty-odd, so far,' he said. 'They're just sketches.'

On each sheet, and on top of this newsprint ground, he had drawn Thatcher's face over and over again, using the grey and the black of the newsprint as a kind of ready-made shading, and working into this to create highlights with, what was it? Just white paint? No, he'd been using a combination: some sort of black pastel or crayon *and* the white paint.

However, looking more closely, Laura suddenly noticed that actually any real or substantial likeness was a kind of illusion. None of Jeremy's drawings, if you could even really call them that, showed the entirety of that all too hideously familiar head; far from it. One just meticulously picked out the highlights on her pearl necklace in white. Others showed simply a droop of brow, or a hint of jowl. Here was a slow curve of hair-sprayed coiffure, there her dead-eyed gaze.

---

[254]   4 down: 'Senility (6).' #5,012. *Ibid.*
[255]   12 down: 'Ordinary chap (5, 3).' #5,012. *Ibid.*

In fact, now that Laura looked from one single drawing to another, and on around the room, she could see that in each case there was literally almost nothing there. Just a page of newsprint and a splash of white paint, or a line or two of black crayon. And yet somehow, stepping back and seeing them all together, the absolute likeness was unmistakeable.

Perhaps, Laura thought, this optical illusion was the product of some cumulative act of memory and cognition that allowed the image to be constructed from one drawing to another as with the flickering projection, frame by frame, of a film on to a cinema screen. If not that, then maybe it was something to do with the power of caricature, or with the persistence of vision and the steady accretion of detail. Or perhaps, and most likely of all, it was none of these things, but simply some inevitable effect of the familiarity of her image that created the illusion of continuity.

Afterword

Dicky Star and the garden rule was commissioned alongside and to form a critical response to the remarkable body of research and creative works currently being produced and exhibited by the artists Jane and Louise Wilson, who themselves are responding to and investigating the Chernobyl disaster of 1986 for a major commission and series of exhibitions that began at the John Hansard Gallery, Southampton in 2011 and continues at Dundee Contemporary Arts and the Whitworth Art Gallery, University of Manchester through 2012.

The story occupies the Chernobyl time-line, from 26 April 1986 when the accident occurred, until 7 May when reports of the true scale of the disaster were printed in UK newspapers following the Kremlin press conference of the previous day. Rather than work with Jane and Louise in Ukraine or to have drawn too heavily upon the unique interviews and testimonies that they have been collecting in the course of their own research, it seemed pertinent to explore, in a work of fiction, the same events from a UK perspective and using contemporary print media as my primary source.

A metaphor for this approach might be that of the scientific control. In an experiment – e.g. one designed to test the effects of a particular drug – the control is of course the experimental sample that remains untreated or subject only to some standard or pre-existing variable or attribute in contrast to, or to provide a point of comparison with the main, treated sample.

My own research draws on two main sources. Firstly, the *Leeds Other Paper* archive, which is held in the local and family history section of Leeds Central Library. *LOP* was an independent, alternative left-wing newspaper published between 1974 and 1994 in that city, where I lived during the period in question. Secondly, archive copies of *The Guardian* newspaper held in the British Library's national newspaper collection at Colindale, London.

I am also indebted, as ever, to the writings of Michael Moorcock. As noted by a character in the text, *The Guardian* book page (singular) of Thursday 1st May 1986 includes a review by Robert Nye of a then new Michael Moorcock novel, *The City in the Autumn Stars*. This is the sequel to an earlier novel by Michael Moorcock, 1981's *The Warhound and the World's Pain*, in whose pages my character Jeremy finds what seem like eerie predictions of the Chernobyl disaster. These few short and prophetic-seeming passages are quoted here (on pages 18, 19 and 43) exactly as found in Michael Moorcock's work. (Further bibliographical information in 'Notes' below.)

Alongside the *Leeds Other Paper*'s prior anti-nuclear content, its critical stance and its notable dissemination of accurate scientific information about risks posed by 'the cloud' (as the plume of Chernobyl fallout was popularly referred to at the time), and *The Guardian*'s own extensive coverage of the disaster, I was particularly drawn to the then broadsheet's back pages, to Steve Bell's memorable cartoons of radioactive sheep and to the two crosswords, especially the Quick

Crossword which I had been fond of doing at the time.

I was mindful of Jane and Louise Wilson's eloquent deployment here of the (actual rather than metaphorical) yardstick – a legacy of their work in the Stanley Kubrick archive – and thinking too of the experimental literary strategies and constraints used by the French writer and novelist Georges Perec (1936-1982) and the other members of Oulipo, the *Ouvroir de littérature potentielle*. During the later years of his life, Perec composed a weekly crossword for the news magazine *Le Point*. Might *The Guardian* crosswords themselves, I wondered, synthesise both of these imperitives? Could they be used to provide meter (in a loosely poetic sense) and measure, *as well as* a useful literary constraint, a mandated vocabulary that might form in effect the tightly controlled variable needed for a literary if not a scientific control? *Dicky Star and the garden rule* was written to test that proposition.

In following the Chernobyl timeline then, this story is structured as a series of daily chapters running from 26 April to 7 May 1986 (*Guardian* days only, so excluding Sundays), the course of each of which (including the names of the two main characters) was determined by its own puzzle: that without going 'off subject' and as economically as possible it had to incorporate every answer to that day's Quick Crossword, each of which I completed before beginning to write.

The title is itself adapted from a speculative, crossword-style clue of my own, which also relates to these works of Jane and Louise Wilson and might alternatively be expressed as follows: Dicky Star (anag) – garden rule? (9).

Tony White, Oxford, January 2012

Notes

i   Margaret Thatcher, 23 September 1987, 'Interview for *Woman's Own* ("no such thing as society")', excerpt of interview transcript available at Margaret Thatcher Foundation website http://www.margaretthatcher.org/speeches/displaydocument.asp?docid=106689

ii   Quick Crossword 5,003. *The Guardian* 26 April 1986.

iii   #5,003. *The Guardian. Ibid.*

iv   #5,003. *The Guardian. Ibid.*

v   #5,003. *The Guardian. Ibid.*

vi   #5,003. *The Guardian. Ibid.*

vii   David Fairhall, 'Radioactive Russian dust cloud escapes: Scandinavia feels effects of power plant accident', *The Guardian*, Tuesday 29 April 1986, p.1.

viii David Fairhall, Martin Walker, 'Russia admits blast as death fears rise: Reactor region evacuated as Moscow appeals for Western help,' *The Guardian*, Wednesday 30 April 1986, p.1

ix   David Fairhall, Martin Walker, *Ibid.*

x   Martin Walker, 'Silence covers "zone of death"', *The Guardian*, Wednesday 30 April 1986, p.1

xi   Michael Moorcock, *The Warhound and the World's Pain*, in *Von Bek*, London: Millennium. p.10

xii   Michael Moorcock, *Ibid.* p.11

xiii Michael Moorcock, *Ibid.* p.11

xiv 'Photograph of the Chernobyl nuclear plant taken from the February edition of Soviet Life magazine,' *The Guardian*, Wednesday 30 April 1986, p.1

xv   Michael Moorcock, *op. cit.* p.11

xvi   Michael Moorcock, *op. cit.* p.11-12

xvii Robert Nye, 'Glorious parody,' *The Guardian*, Thursday 1 May 1986. p.20

xviii Michael White, Martin Walker, Alex Brummer, 'US estimates up to 3,000 victims from satellite information', *The Guardian*, Thursday 1 May 1986, p.1.

xix   Quick Crossword 5,011. *The Guardian*, 6 May 1986

xx   'Solutions No. 5011' in Quick Crossword 5,012. *The Guardian*, 7 May 1986.

xxi   Michael Moorcock, *op. cit.* p.57

xxii Michael Moorcock, *op. cit.* p.57

Tony White

Tony White is a writer and author of novels including *Foxy-T* (Faber and Faber). He has recently been writer in residence at the Science Museum, London and Leverhulme Trust writer in residence at the UCL School of Slavonic and East European Studies, and is currently chair of Resonance 104.4fm, London's award-winning arts radio station.

In 2010 he collaborated with Blast Theory to write *Ivy4evr*, an interactive, SMS-based, mobile phone drama for young people which was commissioned by Channel 4 and broadcast in October 2010. *Ivy4evr* was nominated for a BIMA award in 2011 by the British Interactive Media Association.

Tony White is also the author of the non-fiction work *Another Fool in the Balkans* (Cadogan), editor and co-editor of short story collections including *Croatian Nights* (Serpent's Tail), and his short stories have appeared in numerous publications, journals, collections and exhibition catalogues. Tony White edits and publishes the artists' book imprint Piece of Paper Press which he founded in 1994. His blog is at http://pieceofpaperpress.wordpress.com